Agei

Fallen Fathers

Treena Wynes

Chapter 1

The alley was dark. So much so that, maybe whoever this guy was, he wouldn't find him in there. Could he take the chance? Javier looked over his shoulder, and the long tunnel of dark alley stretched out before him, terminating in a spot of light from the street with which it intersected. It wasn't as busy as it usually was, so every footstep echoed like someone was smashing a hammer against an anvil.

They were getting closer, whoever they were. Javier's lungs burned, and his heart ached, but he had to keep going. This guy was big and angry, and he had eyes that glowed red in the night. Javier had seen that from the other side of the bar. The way those eyes burned into him...how uncanny they looked.

He shook the image out of his head. He'd been running for six blocks now, and whoever this guy was, he seemed to be able to catch up to him without breaking a sweat. It was almost—he didn't wanna think like this—but it was almost as if the guy was *toying* with him. And now, as Javier came up to the chain-link fence at the end of the alley and tried the doors to buildings on both sides of him—all of which were locked—he wondered how much of this was part of the creep's plan.

The laughter that came from behind him said everything. Javier closed his eyes.

"Which demon are you?" he said.

"One looking for something. Something very valuable. And I think you know what it is."

In the darkness, the man seemed even taller. It may have been a trick of the light—of the dark, even—but he seemed to come up to maybe seven feet and had muscle to fill out that tall frame. His jaw, too, was carved out of stone and didn't seem to be moving when he spoke.

The words, Javier noted, seemed to be coming from inside his head...

"It's you," Javier said. "But...you're too early."

"That's not what I've been told. And who would know better than I? I have a direct connection to The Man Downstairs."

"You can't actually think I'll do this." Javier took a step back. The demon was getting closer...*too* close. "Nobody's gonna help you out. We'd all sooner die."

"Death is the least of your worries. Believe me."

Javier backed up into the fence, which jangled behind him. It was getting to where there was no way out, nowhere to go, and not enough room to sneak around him.

But that couldn't be it. He couldn't be stuck like this, now, where his only option was to give up. What was around them? Rats scurried along the wet ground, running into garbage bags that lined the alley. The bags were all over the place, but they'd be no good.

Except there was a garbage bin. It was a long shot and right in between Javier and the demon. It wouldn't do much good, but might just be enough of a weapon to push the demon away or even stun him for a second.

The demon laughed. Javier clenched his jaw, pushed back into his heels, and lunged forward, grabbing hold of the garbage can which only made the demon laugh harder, even as Javier picked it up and smashed it into the demon's side, where it was swatted away like it was made of paper.

Still, it had been just enough for Javier to sneak past him. It was a long way to the end of the alley, but he was pushing as hard as he could. He was sure he could make it, he'd get to the end of the—

The demon was right in front of him.

How'd he do that?! How'd he move so fast?! Javier couldn't stop himself. He ran right smack into the demon and fell backwards onto his arm, which bent unnaturally behind him as he landed on it.

The snap of his bone echoed. It was sickening, but the feeling was much worse. Javier propped himself up using his good arm and spat onto the ground, not sure if he was gonna vomit or not.

They'd said this demon could teleport; that he spoke with his mind and was tall and obedient, calculating. He was the best soldier the other side had. Was it all true? Wasn't this just a myth?

"I know what you're thinking," the demon said. "I am real. This is happening. You're going to talk."

"What'll you do if I don't? You know they're coming for you either way."

"Why shouldn't they?" the demon replied. He picked Javier up by the collar and shoved him into the wall...*hard*...jostling his brain. "It's what I'd do if I was them. Now, tell me where I can find him."

"Find who?"

The demon's eyes glowed. He clutched Javier's throat, and immediately, Javier lost his peripheral vision. His lungs burned, begging for air.

"They said you had him," Javier said. "What happened? Did you lose him?"

"Are you saying nobody told you?"

"Please—I can't breathe..."

"You were his best friend," the demon whispered. "He hasn't contacted you even *once*?"

"I don't...I can't..."

His vision went even blacker. His limbs twitched. He tried smacking the demon's hands away, but they were mountains closing in on his throat. In that moment, he would have told the demon anything, but Baraqiel hadn't sought him out, not that he knew of, anyway.

Why couldn't it have been so? If Baraqiel had found him, Javier could have given his friend up and lived. It wasn't fair...to die like this.

The last thing he heard was the laughing coming from his assailant. Then, his limbs finally gave out on him, and he hung limp. Everything became nothing.

***

If only there was something he could've done. If only there was some way he could've jumped in and saved his friend without compromising himself. Instead, he looked around the corner and into the alley, hiding his form as best he could, until Javier was dropped, and the demon abandoned Javier's body to the rats.

Baraqiel—Barry—left the alley and walked, quickly, but trying to blend in, too. He wore the garb of what people here would call a homeless man: torn clothes and a towel as a hood, all of which was moldy and stank to high heaven. He effected a limp, which he prayed was convincing, but there was no way of knowing for sure.

No matter; it wouldn't fool him. The demon had seen Barry try everything to get away from him. He'd seen him try to fake his own death for God's sake. The limp wouldn't fool the demon, but it might fool a Viper who wasn't looking properly.

Javier was obviously gonna be of no help to him now. He'd have to find some other way of getting out of this and fast.

It was then that someone approached him, reaching into his pocket. The man was tall, blonde, talking to his wife, and getting ready to throw Barry a few bucks. Barry waved his hand to say it was okay; he didn't want any, but the man grabbed hold of his sleeve to hold him into place.

"Hold on a sec," the man said, and then turned to his wife. "You see, honey? A little kindness goes a long way. If I can just get my...Hold on..."

"I'm okay," Barry said. "Really. I *just* ate."

"You'll need to eat again soon. Sorry, it's just—I have a habit of putting garbage in my pockets. Isn't that right, dear?"

"It's true," the man's wife replied. "You should see how big his pockets—oh my word, that's a tall man. Honey, you see him?"

Oh no.

The demon was standing at the edge of the alley, looking around, sniffing as though he smelled something familiar. Barry didn't have but two seconds to get away.

"I don't want any money," Barry said, feeling panic start to rise in his gut. "I just want you to let me go."

"We've already come this far," the man insisted. "Plus, I like to help. Really, it's no sweat."

"But I can't be here. Do you understand me? You have to—will you just let go of my arm?"

"Throw me a bone here, wouldja? I'm trying to impress my wife with how generous I am—"

"Listen to me," Barry said, his tone becoming serious. "I'd pull away from you, but I don't wanna cause a scene. And you seem like the kinda guy who takes everything personally." He paused, looking over to the man's wife, "Am I wrong?"

"That's true," she said, fear showing in her voice.

"I don't want your money. I don't care about your wife. I want you to let me go, and if you don't, or if you make a scene in any way, you'll regret it. That's a promise."

The man stood stark still for a moment. It was as though he couldn't tell if Barry was kidding or not, but soon enough, he released Barry's arm and nodded that he was gonna be cool.

That was good...because the demon's footsteps were getting closer. Maybe in that time, he'd found Barry out. It was hard to say without turning around and exposing himself, so he trudged forward, conscious of the footsteps gaining on him, praying under his breath and hoping someone would take pity on him—

Barry turned down the nearest alley and forced himself to vomit. He spoke gibberish to himself, laughing and feeling the presence of the demon on the other side of him, hearing the scoffing laughter as the demon found himself amused by the wretched state of human life.

Luckily, the demon continued on his way. Barry sighed, peered around the corner, and saw the tall man walking in the other direction. He leaned against the wall and closed his eyes.

He just *had* to get away. For however long that took, it didn't matter. He was done fighting. He was worn, exhausted, and angry, and he didn't have any energy left.

Too bad. Because if the demon *did* find him...it was gonna mean the end of the world.

Chapter 2

It was getting colder outside every day. The grass was turning beige, and every morning, his nose would burn right around his nostrils from where the air hit it. A tightness came across his skin that made him wonder why he stayed in cold country year after year. Even the heat from his coffee was more painful than comforting, and while the outside of his hands recoiled from the cold, the palms screamed that he should've let the mug sit a few more minutes before he came outside.

Even the warm air from inside, which touched him a moment as the front door opened, was more of a tease than anything, and it was quickly replaced with Lucas sighing and leaning on the porch railing next to him. There was a look on his face like he couldn't believe he was still out in God's country, which had Marco rolling his eyes. It wasn't *that* good—honestly. It was still damn cold.

"You seen her yet?" Lucas asked before taking a sip from his own steaming mug.

"Not yet. Car's not in, either."

"She handles the temptation pretty well."

"It's remarkable, don't you think?"

Lucas smiled and nodded, then looked back out over the field. He'd been putting all of them up at his place ever since the incident with Little Johnnie the year before, which was nice of him. But what was that look about? It was a knowing glance, wasn't it?

"You've been looking at her different," Lucas said.

"No. I don't—I haven't. Why?"

"Nothing."

"Did she say something, or—?"

"About what?" Lucas asked. "You?"

"About me looking at her."

"No. But I'm getting the impression she's lonely."

Marco had been thinking the same thing. She'd been going out more, staying out later. Last night, she'd spent a good chunk of time pacing around, giving short answers when anyone spoke to her. When she finally went out, it was like someone had been shaking a soda bottle, and the lid had flown off.

"Do you think she's out there looking for someone?" Marco asked.

"Jealous?"

"Maybe I'm just looking for someone to look after. Little Johnnie's been back home a long time. Or—you're looking at me funny."

"It's a nice excuse," Lucas said, patting him on the back. "Anyway, I'm sure she's fine. It's not like she can't get herself out of trouble."

Fair enough...but something didn't quite sit right with Marco. He didn't even feel Lucas' hand pat him on the back before he went inside, because whatever it was, it sat right on the tip of his tongue, a taste in the air.

Maybe it was in the breeze that washed over the dying grass. Or maybe it was that half-angel empathy going into overdrive. Whatever the case, something was wrong, or something was *going* wrong, and he didn't have the faintest idea what exactly it was.

***

Purple lights flashed across the grimy floor and lit up a sea of pale, unsmiling faces with red lipstick smeared across their cheeks and black hair that draped over their eyes. It was deafening. Computer beats spat out mechanical noises like hammers smashing against garbage cans in endless repetition, distorted voices screeched about melancholy, surgery...The smell was of leather and dust, and the place was called 'Dracula's'.

It was even cold in there. That, plus the cramped quarters, was like being inside an industrial grave. It was a comforting feeling, dancing among the living dead, and she couldn't help but smile, even if that was strictly verboten. What did it matter that smiling wasn't 'goth' enough?

Diamond stepped out from the dance floor and approached the bar to order a water. Her brain didn't think about alcohol in the same way anymore—she didn't imagine herself asking for a drink. She didn't have to control the words before they came out of her mouth and ended in something awkward, like, "I'm sorry, I didn't mean to order this." She just ordered the water, hydrated, wiped sweat from her brow, and got a good look at the dancing goths as they shifted their weight from one leg to another. It made her laugh—any more complicated moves than that and you'd be a 'normie'. The owner would probably never let you back inside.

"Excuse me?" someone said behind her. "Do I know you from somewhere?"

She didn't turn around. She just said, "Is that the best you've got?", and whoever it was didn't answer. Diamond could feel his disappointment and sensed him walking away from her, but she didn't care. The guys at home seemed to think she was lonely, but that was crap. Utter *crap*. She just needed to get away every once in a while, meet someone who wasn't—

Someone in the crowd was looking at her. He was the one, still face; the only one facing her while everyone looked towards the DJ. That face was angular and pale, neither of which separated him from the others, but the genuine intensity of his gaze—was that it? It couldn't have been all.

She stared back. She couldn't help it. And when he stepped towards her, she wanted so badly to avert her eyes, except that she was sucked in, breathing deeply.

He separated from the crowd and stood a few feet in front of her. He was tall and intense. Byronic, even.

"Aren't your friends gonna wonder where you are?" Diamond asked.

"There is pleasure in the pathless woods," he said. "There is rapture in the lonely shore; there is society where none intrudes, by the deep sea, and music in its roar."

"You even quote Byron. Don't you think you're a little on the nose?"

He smiled, and it chilled her heart. "I like my solitude. I didn't come here with anyone."

"And you won't be leaving here with anyone, *either*. Unless you have someone else in mind."

He was about to say something, maybe about how he had no one else in mind at all, when a Rivethead, wearing a long trench coat, big boots, and a gas mask, came up from behind him and placed a hand on his shoulder.

It was obvious what was about to happen. Diamond set her water down and took a gingerly step from off her stool, right as the Rivethead pulled off his gas mask to reveal the tight, jaw-chewing face of a man who'd taken something dangerous tonight.

"I've never seen you around here before," the Rivethead said. "What's your name?"

"Tyreal," the man said. "'Ty', if you like. And what do I call you?"

"I don't think you belong here."

"Is this the part where you call me a poser?"

Diamond had to admit, Ty *didn't* look like he belonged. He was wearing a fitted grey blazer over a white T-shirt, for one, and while his pants were black, they were obviously jeans. Not to mention, he had on some pricey-looking sneakers; Gucci, she suspected.

"Why don't you go back to—"

The Rivethead didn't get the next word out, because before anyone could blink, Ty had him on the ground in an arm-bar that was threatening to snap his forearm in half.

There was a commotion. Two guys must have seen Ty throw their friend on the ground, because they tapped each other on the shoulder and approached with their fists at the ready. Diamond made a quick motion around Ty and held up her hands to the Rivethead's friends to stop them.

"Let it go," she said, the tone in her voice clear that she wasn't gonna take any crap from them.

Neither of them wanted to listen. One of them pushed her out of the way with a laugh, but she grabbed him by the wrist and flung him over her shoulder and onto the ground with a smack that was audible above even the music.

This was gonna get bad.

Ty kicked the Rivethead in the jaw to knock him unconscious and then got up and hit the next closest person before all hell broke loose. Even as the music continued, goths everywhere were leaping into this mass of bodies, swinging fists and clawing at each other while Diamond pushed as many of them out of the way as she could, and Ty threw his hands at whoever came too close to him.

Once the music stopped, that was enough. She ran for the door with Ty beside her, broke out into the cool morning sun, and couldn't help herself—she laughed.

Ty didn't. He caught his breath and looked down the stairs towards the door to Dracula's, as if waiting for someone else to pop out.

"Where'd you learn to do that?" he said.

"I have a few tricks up my sleeve. You wanna get out of here?"

For a moment, he only looked down the stairs. The noise of the fight was getting closer to the door. As it grew louder and louder, his eyes widened, his hands clenched into fists, and his body tensed.

Did he wanna fight? What was she gonna do—fight alongside him? But before she could do anything, the door flew open. A terrified man ran up the steps, hyperventilating, with a cut on his forehead and a swollen lip that'd hurt in the morning.

She wanted to reach out and help him, but Ty pulled his fist back and pummeled it into the man's face. The guy tumbled backwards and down the stairs before landing in front of the door, his eyes closed.

"What'd you do?" Diamond asked, shocked and frantic.

She ran down the stairs and picked him up and over her arm, feeling for a pulse and finding one, strong, as he unconsciously breathed onto her neck. She took him up the stairs where Ty was still standing, immovable.

She set the man down at the top of the stairs and against the wall, checked his pulse again, and relaxed—he was fine, just unconscious.

"Come on," Ty said. "Let's get out of here."

All of her feelings gave way to repulsion. Ty had hit this man for no reason, but the rage that came out of him was thick like miasma. She didn't wanna go with him. She had a feeling that things would get bad around here and that she could help.

Diamond didn't wanna follow Ty. She wanted to be anywhere else. She was, in a way, *terrified* by him. But there'd be trouble coming out that door any second; plus, it was morning.

She wasn't lonely, but she followed him away from the club, anyway.

Chapter 3

The wood exploded, splintering into a thousand pieces that shot in every direction like a pulpy mist fired from a canon. Diamond landed on her feet with one hand to the floor in a runner's position. She then kicked herself up and corkscrewed towards the next log, the one which stood three feet off to her left. Her left wing through the wood, cutting it in half so quickly the two pieces stayed perfectly balanced on top of each other until her feet swung around and tossed the top half off and into the wall.

When she landed that time, she did so in a standing position with her hands on her hips. It wasn't exhausting this time around either—she was barely out of breath, not like when she'd started this all those months ago. She barely even noticed Marco clapping from the stairs, smiling at her, and standing up to examine the busted pieces of wood strewn about all over the floor to Lucas' cellar.

"Not bad," he said. "Did any of them put up a fight at least?"

"Hardly. Did you see the one I exploded? Boom! What about you? Want a turn?"

Marco waved dismissively. He'd been experimenting with his own wings lately, but he hadn't quite got the hang of them yet. Not that long ago, he'd figured out how to get them to flap real fast, which would probably come in handy at some point—get a strong wind going to toss some bad guys away like rag dolls; that is, if he could get them going fast enough, obviously.

But this confused Diamond. Why didn't he wanna try them out *now*? Was he embarrassed? She'd done a pretty slick job of tearing those logs apart, imagining they were Vipers, and countering imagined moves in her mind. Maybe it freaked him out knowing how good she was getting.

There was no point in pressing it. Plus, she had somewhere to be. She smiled at Marco and went to move past him when he coughed and pointed with his chin towards something at the other end of the cellar.

What was it—oh, well, it was just a lonely log sitting at the far end. She must have missed it. She shrugged and said, "It gets to live," but Marco ducked past her and walked over to stand beside it.

"This one?" he asked, pretending to examine it. "This is one of the Dark Ones. You don't wanna let this one live, or he'll kill us all!"

"Come on. Look at all his henchman—if he's not running scared, he's stupid enough to get himself killed tying his shoelaces."

"I dunno—"

"I've got somewhere to be, man. Maybe you should practice on it."

"You have somewhere to—"

"Yeah," she said, "A date. Don't look at me like that; he's a nice guy. I met him when I was out the other day. I gave him my number, and—what? What's wrong?" Marco was giving her a weird look.

"Is it a good idea to be hanging out with strange men like that?"

"What am I, a child? He's harmless. If he tries to give me candy out of his van, I'll make sure to kick the crap out of him."

Something was up with Marco that she couldn't read. Was it—what, nervousness? Was he scared of her winding up with someone dangerous?

"Did you not see what I just did to these things?" she asked, gesturing to the splintery carnage around them. "I can handle myself."

"Yeah, you were good. But these things don't fight back."

"Night Adder wasn't a log."

"No," Marco said, "but it's been a while since Night Adder. Aren't you worried you're out of practice?"

Okay, *now* she had to roll her eyes. What was his problem? For starters, she wasn't 'out of practice'. She'd been testing her abilities almost every day since she won the fight against Night Adder, and second, even if she *hadn't*, maybe Ty was a bit edgy, but she could obviously take him in a fight even without her wings.

It was a done deal.

Yet Marco had this look about him like he wanted to stop her from going out and—frankly—it was more than a little insulting. He was acting like this a lot lately, kinda cozying up to her and whatever, and sure, it was nice having him around, but she didn't need an older brother.

There'd been a time right around when she'd gotten out of rehab where she'd been kinda restless. She wasn't used to being cooped up inside all the time; she was used to going out, seeing people, getting in trouble...like, *really* getting into trouble. And that was maybe the weirdest part for her: it's not just how pleasurable it was being face-first in muck, being stuck in some place that felt genuinely awful, but how much she missed it when it wasn't around anymore.

Marco must have noticed this, because one day, he came up into her room and knocked on the door. She was lying on her back with her arms and legs splayed out, staring through the ceiling with her mouth hanging open and groaning with a hint of vocal fry in the sound.

"I'm so bored," she said.

"Why? Because you're not throwing up in the back of a cop car?"

"Do you know what I'd be doing right now if it wasn't for rehab? I *would* be throwing up in the back of a cop car."

"You weren't listening to me, obviously."

"Did you say something?"

Marco sat down at the edge of her bed. Maybe he hadn't realized it, but his leg touched hers, and for a moment, she wanted to pull away, but—she also didn't, at the same time? If that makes sense? Anyway, she left it just where it was and wondered if he'd figure that out.

"Why don't we go for a walk?" he suggested. "Just the two of us. Outside."

"Can we fight somebody while we're on this walk?"

"No. Who would we fight, anyway?"

"I dunno. Farmers. Come on, man, you know I'm not a country gal. What am I supposed to do on this walk?"

"Why don't you come and find out?"

Well, she had to admit—the first part of it *sucked*. It was so boring, but once the two of them got going, she kinda calmed down a bit and started noticing little things, like the circular hay bales, whatever you called those. They looked nice, lying out, speckling the fields. And the cows that grazed and the horses, well, she liked the horses.

But most of all, it was something about Marco. He was such a comforting presence; the way he kept his hands jammed into his pockets, and the calmness in his voice when she'd talk about things she used to get up to in the city.

"You really threw a guy through a wall?"

"Sure," she said. "I was drunk at the time. And in fairness to me, he was being all creepy and weird and—you know the type? Anyway, yeah, picked him up and threw him through a wall."

"And what about the bar? Did they ever let you back?"

"I can't remember. I may have gone back there once or twice, but if they let me in, it was only because they were afraid."

This made her laugh for a moment until the separation between who she was before and who she was now dawned on her. It really *was* like being a whole other person. That person who'd said she was only interested in Marco as a friend—the one who'd thought she'd had a crush on the guy but had changed her mind after rehab—maybe that was another person, too. Maybe she really did have something like feelings for him.

Or maybe not "something like" at all. Maybe she was just putting distance between herself and how she felt about him.

But by the time they got back Lucas' and walked up the steps, those feelings went away. Where they went, she wasn't sure, but they'd been strong only a little while ago, and you know, maybe the wind took them away or something, because now she was standing with him on the porch and that urge she had to touch his arm was a thing of the past.

She just wanted him to know how much better she felt.

"I'm glad," he said. "Sometimes simple things can be nice like that. It's not always about adrenaline and fighting, drinking and drugs."

"Not always. But sometimes."

He knew she was kidding. She could tell by that eye-roll laugh of his. He was perceptive, so empathetic. It must have been the angel in him—or maybe not. Maybe he was just like this.

They went for walks like that as often as she needed. And after every one of them, she knew that he was the best friend she'd ever had. Which was all it was—that she enjoyed his company and wanted to spend time with him, but always in a platonic sense, because he made her feel good; feel comfortable being herself.

However, those walks had turned into something more filial than they used to be.

And it wasn't what she needed right now.

"I'm bothering you, aren't I?" Marco asked.

"I've been cooped up in this house for months. You guys are great, but you're everywhere. Ty's something different. Plus, he's—I dunno, maybe you guys would get along."

Marco opened his mouth to respond, but a car pulled up outside. The headlights flooded through the cellar windows and a horn honked. Industrial music was audible but muffled, and Diamond could kinda hear someone say, "Hey! Where are you? I don't have all day!"

Whatever. Marco could play the "big brother" to somebody else. She didn't need that. She waved to him and ran up the steps to the outside and threw open the door to find Ty sitting with his arm around the headrest of his seat.

He looked *good*. She hadn't noticed his hazel eyes before, but something about the light when she got into the passenger side really brought them out. She said "Hi", but he didn't say a word in response.

He just put the car in reverse and pulled out of the driveway, cranked the music up, and drove off into the night.

***

They'd never find him here. At least, not yet. He leaned against one of the big cedars to catch his breath, closed his eyes, and took in the sounds of the forest, from animals jumping from one branch to the next, to crickets, to something walking across the fallen and dried leaves.

But no sound of anyone pursuing him.

Good. He could rest a moment.

He sat down and used the cedar to support his back as he tried to figure out what he was gonna do next. Nobody'd let him stay at their house, not with the way he looked. If he'd looked homeless the night before, he'd only gotten worse, what with his running through the woods and hiding in alleys and everything. And it's not like there were any clothing stores all the way out here, away from civilization.

Which meant either the demon would for sure be looking for him out here or wouldn't suspect that he'd gone all this way. The smart move may have been to hide in plain sight, but it was hard to tell with that guy. He was experienced and ruthless. Everyone was terrified of him and for good reason. What 'outsmarting' him meant wasn't clear.

Whatever the case, Barry had to stay on the move. He'd rested enough as it was. He got back on his feet, dusted himself off, and breathed deep as a shooting star shot across the sky, careening past the endless array of stars and then disappeared.

Was anyone from up there watching him? It had been so long, maybe they'd forgotten. Maybe they'd abandoned him. That was what it meant to be on his own—to be *really* on his own; abandoned by the cosmos with no one to help him because nobody cared.

That was all he'd felt when he'd been chained up in that room all those years, barely alive, dreaming of escape only until it seemed impossible. And then he'd dreamed only of death. Anything to escape the terrible laughter, the din of those sycophantic libertines with their bacchanalian rites and their disgusting, feigned affection for one another...

Where was God when they'd poured boiling water on him? When they'd pressed hot pokers into his skin, read from insane and dark grimoires to possess him with a spirit of pain, and then left that spirit in him for six whole months before it got tired and left of its own accord? What about when—

But why dwell on it? It was over now.

That he'd escaped at all had been a miracle in itself. He wasn't supposed to get out. Except that somebody had taken pity on him and at the perfect time, too—right as all Hell was gonna break loose...*literally*. It just would have been nice if his escape had meant *something*, if it meant a moment of rest instead of the endless panic of pursuit, waiting for something to happen, for someone to find him.

A twig snapped from somewhere behind him. It didn't startle him like it maybe should have, but it *did* fill him with a feeling like annoyance, a feeling like frustration, a sensation like wondering when this was gonna be over.

Not yet, it looked like.

He pushed off from the ground into a jog and hoped that whatever happened, some solution, *somewhere*, would present itself.

Because, frankly, he was out of ideas. And a lot was riding on him coming up with a plan.

Chapter 4

Was something running through the woods? It was hard to tell at night, but Diamond could swear she felt all the life out there—something about that empathic response she'd been honing that sensed in some immaterial way that there were things out there, things that felt hunger and fear and wanted to hide. And something else, although she couldn't quite place it.

Ty didn't seem to notice, but *of course* he didn't. He was sitting in the driver's seat at the edge of the woods, looking out at the expanse of trees like he'd been promised something that hadn't happened. It was difficult getting a conversation going with him. He'd just kinda sat there the whole time...?

"Is this really what you wanted to do?" Diamond asked. "Stare into the woods?"

"I don't wanna go out."

"Why?"

"Because. You know...maybe this was a bad idea."

"Do you wanna be alone?"

He rolled his eyes. She wasn't gonna get a response from him, so she leaned back into the seat as he started the engine. What a waste of time this turned out to be.

"Where do you live?" she asked.

"Why do you ask?"

"Because if you're not gonna say anything, I think I'd rather walk."

For a moment, he kept his hands on the ignition. It was hard to tell, but she wondered if maybe he was thinking about—was he second-guessing leaving? He made a horse sound with his lips, turned the engine off, and ran his hands through his hair like he was frustrated.

Why was this so difficult for him? And why'd he wanna come all the way out here, anyway?

"I live, um...outside of town," he said. "In a big mansion on a hill."

"Really?"

"Don't look at me like that. I didn't wanna say anything—"

"Rich boy, huh? Wait, wait—sorry, I didn't mean to insult you. Don't turn the engine on. Okay, let's try this then: who do you live with?"

"My dad...and some other people."

"Who are these other people?"

"I don't know. No, seriously, I have *no idea*. I've never met any of them. I've never even..."

"What?" Diamond could practically see the flower ready to open up. She leaned in closer, anticipating that he might be quiet.

"You probably know your dad super well."

"I've never met him. Really."

"You're lucky," Ty said. "Dads can be a pain in the ass."

It was impossible to deny that something passed between them. The scowl that Ty wore fell away and something like a young boy emerged, one that never got to say what he needed to say about his dad, about *anything*. It was sad, and there was a sadness to him that lurked underneath the cold surface.

She saw herself reaching for his arm and placing her fingers around his bicep, leaning her head against his shoulder, and sitting there in the quiet. They let the cricket sounds pass overhead and around them, waiting until the time felt right to go home. Was he thinking about that? Or was it something else?

She reached up for him, but in that moment, his expression changed—it started in his eyes: they narrowed and focused. His hands gripped the steering wheel, and his lips flattened. Whatever had been exposed was gone, and it made Diamond recoil with how quickly it happened.

Did he just turn himself off?

"What's wrong?" she asked.

"Look," he said and got out of the car. Diamond did the same.

There was a tree not six feet in front of where they were parked, a big oak tree that was blackened by the night but sort of visible around its edges. Ty was looking at something at its base, something she couldn't see, but which brought a smile to his face that made her wanna turn and run.

"Can't you hear it?" he asked. "Squeaking. Look, there."

He pointed, and although it took a second for her eyes to adjust, the bat with the broken wing revealed itself. She gasped, held her hands to her mouth and bent down—as if she missed this, with all her empathy, the poor hurt thing crawling at the base of the tree.

But that didn't seem to be what Ty was feeling. That smile of his really *was* wicked...

"We have to take it to the vet," Diamond said. "Come on, I know just the one."

"The vet? For this thing?" Then he said to the bat, "How's it feel, huh? Does it hurt?"

"Of course it—what are you doing?"

He was laughing, that's what he was doing. Laughing. When this poor thing was crawling across the ground with a busted wing, he was holding his stomach, tilting his head back, and *laughing*.

Whatever came through her, it came in a jet stream. It started deep within her stomach and then erupted out into her shoulders, down into her feet as she pushed herself towards him and landed both hands on his chest, catching him off-balance and nearly forcing him onto his back.

The laughter stopped like someone had flipped a switch. He was like a child who'd been told to stop grabbing the family cat by the tail, like he'd been betrayed by someone who should've let him act on his impulses.

"That's not funny," he said.

"You're driving me to that vet," Diamond said, her tone deadly serious, "or I'm gonna whoop your ass and take it there myself."

Ty tucked his tongue into his cheek and nodded. It looked like he might fight back, but he put his hands up in surrender and got back into the car.

The poor bat. Diamond picked it up gently, ignoring the engine turning on and the horn honking. The bat was hesitant, of course, but she was calm and spoke in a hushed voice until it relented and laid still in her hand. She stroked its head all the way to the vet and didn't say a word to Ty, who, in fairness, didn't say anything back either.

***

When Ty dropped her off at home, they hadn't spoken a word to each other in at least half an hour. The vet had been grateful and said she could absolutely help the animal, who'd be out and himself in no time. It had just dislocated its wing, so it wasn't in any danger of dying—at least, not with the proper care.

That was what Diamond was thinking about when her house came up in front of them. Not Ty with all his daddy issues and his apparent inability to express himself emotionally; all his defense mechanisms that made him into an intolerable snot, but the bat—and how it was that Lucas was up so late, sitting on the porch.

Maybe everyone around here was going a little stir-crazy.

Ty stopped the car, and she got out and closed the door before he drove off. It was such a strange feeling; this toss-up between being attracted to him and outright hating him; between knowing she'd never call him again and wondering if he was gonna call her tomorrow.

He just had some things that needed tuning up, that was all. He was kinda—well, "rough around the edges" was probably the best way of putting it. And with all the work she'd done on herself, she could probably help him.

Lucas, however, as she approached the house, seemed to have something else on his mind.

"The date was fine," she said. "I saved a bat. Ty found it—"

"This is the guy? The one from the other night?"

"I've already got one housemate playing big brother; I don't need two. Why are you up so late?"

"Couldn't sleep. Hold on—"

Diamond went inside and almost shut the door in Lucas' face so as to not have to listen to this, but he caught it before it closed and followed her inside. She pulled out a glass from the cupboard and offered him one, to which he said, "Please. Now will you listen to me?"

"Water?"

"You shouldn't hang around with that guy."

"He has a soft side, I swear." She poured two glasses of water and handed one to Lucas. "He was talking about his dad? We've got a few things in common that way."

"Who's his dad? Do you know?"

"That's some desperation in your voice. Hey, maybe his dad's the spirit of Richard Ramirez! Or—who's a good Minnesota serial killer? Has there been one?"

"You're not listening to me."

"The Weepy-Voiced Killer. Remember him?"

"I saw his aura."

That made Diamond stop for a second. She'd almost forgotten that Lucas could see auras; that he'd seen hers and was how he had known she was an angel. Or half-angel. Whatever. Angel*ic*.

And judging by the look on Lucas' face—

"You're lying," she said. "You're lying because you're protective. That's it."

"I wouldn't lie to you. Who's been there for you more than I have? I know why you're going out all the time—"

"I'm not lonely."

"Fine," Lucas said. "But I'm telling you: I saw Ty's aura, and he's demonic."

That word—it was like getting hit in the face with a glass, like he'd chucked his glass of water at her, and it had smashed into her forehead. It couldn't be true. She stumbled back and then groaned, looking up at the ceiling so she didn't have to see Lucas' face, then all at once wound up and threw her own glass into the wall with a scream.

"I know you're lying!" she shouted. "I'd notice if something was off with him."

"I'm gonna get you another glass—"

"Don't come near me."

"What are you gonna do; hit me?"

Diamond wondered if she would. She could already hear his speech: she was half-angel, so she was given to strong emotions, and the romantic feelings she had were overriding her ability to think rationally about what she sensed in someone else...

Blah. Blah. Blah. Blah. Blah.

She didn't have time for this crap. She pushed Lucas out of the way and grabbed his keys off the key rack on her way out the door. He was calling something after her, but all she could think of was getting in the car and getting out of there.

With tears in her eyes, she drove off into the night, not once looking behind her.

Chapter 5

Diamond pushed down on the gas pedal until the engine fought back and brought her speed down. Her palms sweated against the steering wheel and tears came into her eyes, which she wiped away to get a better look at what was ahead of her.

Didn't they trust her? What with all the work she'd been putting in using her empathy—hell, wasn't she just, earlier that day, feeling the emotions of all those living things in the woods? Except...

The bat. She'd missed the bat. But how—

Something showed up in her headlights. She gasped, and the sound filled the car over the sound of the engine. It might have been a deer running out from the woods; it was something; *something* turned its head and looked at her, its eyes shining against the headlights.

She slammed on the break, and the car spun. The wheels caught the gravel and kicked it up in a cloud of dust while her wings shot out to shield her, leaving enough room for her to see and pull on the steering wheel.

Something collided with the side of her car. It jarred the vehicle and sent it spinning around in the opposite direction before it came to a stop. She was holding onto the steering wheel so tight she might have broken it in half. Her breathing was heavy, loud, and a rapid wheeze.

It had to have been a deer. Nothing else would be running around this late at night. But then...why couldn't she open her eyes to look? Why was she praying that nothing worse than a deer had been hit?

Why was she fighting with the memory of a human face looking at her from the middle of the road?

She opened the door and fell out onto the road, coughing. It took a second to get adjusted, but she propped herself up to a standing position, breathed, and turned to face the site of where she'd hit...well...whatever it was that she'd hit. The stars were bright tonight, like a sparkling blanket over the dark trees on both sides, the road jutting right down the center, and the pile of something, some fleshy object, immobile in the middle of the tire tracks.

Her feet started walking before she commanded them to—her body was more curious than she was. She just wanted to go home, to go back in time and not take the car out. The fleshy object, the mound in the middle of the road, was curled up, its back facing her but its legs brought up to its chest. One of its arms extended outright from the top of what must have been its head, while the other one—she couldn't see the other one.

Her breath hitched. Every step closer was worse than the one further away. Her lip quivered. She held out her hand and sobbed, trying to find the words before she said, "Hello?"

She fell to her knees once she was within six feet of it, and there was no doubt anymore. It was a human...a male; a person whom she'd hit, and all because of a stupid emotional moment, because she couldn't handle—

The body groaned. Lightness filled Diamond's chest, and she struggled to her feet before walking around to the front of the body and kneeling down to see the man blinking, opening his eyes. He was older, muscular, and had black hair that hung matted in front of his eyes. By the way he was dressed, he appeared to be some kind of vagrant.

"What happened?" the man asked.

"I—you were hit by a car. Are you okay?"

"I have to get out of here..."

The man pushed himself up onto his feet. Diamond tried to stop him, but he pushed her off, looking all around him in a rapid cycle. It was like someone had been following him, but that must have been the effect of a concussion...right?

"What's your name?" Diamond asked.

"Why? Who are you?"

The man's expression had changed. There was anger in him now, to which Diamond responded by making fists at her sides and saying, "I'm trying to help. You probably have a concussion."

"I can't get concussions."

"Can't—*what*? Look, you've obviously been hit really hard—"

The man grunted and walked away from her towards the woods. At that point—it was more her stubbornness than anything—she followed him, trying to get in front of him while he kept scanning all around for something, then looking up at the stars as if to figure out where exactly he was before taking a stride into the woods.

"Where are you going?" she asked. "You can't just walk away."

"Oh yeah? What are you gonna do about it?"

She smirked. "I don't think you wanna get on my bad side. Believe me."

"I've heard this before, blah blah—you're starting to bother me. I have places to be—or, more accurately, places to *not* be. Do you mind?"

"Is someone after you?"

The man stopped just inside the border of the woods and rolled his eyes. It was an annoying look, she had to admit. What was his game plan here? Walk off into the woods and die?

"You know what? *Yes.* Somebody's after me. And the longer you keep me here, the more likely he is to find me. How's that? Are you satisfied? Any other questions for me, officer?"

"Just one."

"Oh yeah?"

She grabbed him by the wrist and tried pulling him towards the road, but when she did—and she pulled as hard as she could—he was steady as a rock. That didn't make sense. He was even grinning at her, as though he knew this was coming.

She tried again...and with the same result. He was digging his heels into the ground, but it didn't look like by much. What was the matter with this guy?

"Let go," he said, "or you'll regret it."

Huh. Well, *he'd* be the one who regretted saying that, wouldn't he?

She put everything she had into pulling him towards the road, but once the pull motion that started in the soles of her feet came up through her legs and into her twisting torso through her shoulders, and ending in her fingertips, she was hit by a blinding light that made her let go and drop to the ground.

It was painful—someone must have been shining a searchlight onto her. She screamed with pain in her eyes until the light went away just as quickly as it had come, and the figure of the man loomed over top of her.

But he was no man. That much was clear now.

"Leave me alone," the man whispered threateningly. "If you don't, I can do much, *much* worse than that."

He walked off into the darkness while she remained on her knees, pawing at her eyes. It explained everything. Why he lived through getting hit by the car, why she couldn't make him budge...Even why someone might be after him.

It was what came out of his back. There was no other explanation.

He had a pair of wings.

An angel.

***

Diamond burst through the door to Lucas' place and found Lucas and Marco standing around the kitchen, drinking decafs—and from the looks on their faces when she came in—likely talking about her; how they were worried about her or some crap like that.

They made a motion like they were gonna say something, but she cut them off and said, "No time. Something crazy's just happened."

She took them into the living room where they both sat on the couch, and she paced back and forth while explaining the entire thing. Lucas made an attempt to interrupt when she told how she had crashed his car, but she didn't have time to get into that either—and *whatever*, someone would probably get him a new one. Or she would. Or—no, someone else probably would.

Once she got to where the man flashed a blinding light at her and opened his wings, Lucas and Marco were too stunned to say anything. There were several minutes after she finished speaking where the three stood perfectly still, looking at one another to see who was gonna be the first to talk.

"Well?" she asked. "What do we do?"

"You said somebody's after him?" Lucas replied.

"That's what he said."

"Then—huh."

"Right?"

"We have to do something," Marco said. "*Don't we*? I mean, if he's out there and somebody's looking for him—"

"He could be somebody important." Lucas nodded, thinking for a second. "Okay. Mrs. Delphine has access to a database at the clinic. How well do you remember this guy?"

"Couldn't forget him," Diamond said. "You wanna call her or should I?"

If they'd had a car, Lucas explained, they could have driven there to use it themselves. As it stood, nobody wanted to do any walking, so they FaceTimed Mrs. Delphine at what was now four in the morning, hoping she'd understand.

By the look on her face, it was a good thing that this was important.

"It's late." Mrs. Delphine rubbed sleep out of her eyes. It was obvious she slept with a mask on, as well as cream. Diamond didn't wanna laugh, but it was getting hard to stifle. "What do you want?"

Diamond told the story again. Mrs. Delphine's expression changed once Diamond got to where she had hit someone with her car, but once she got to the part where the man had revealed himself to be an angel, *that* was the game-changer.

Mrs. Delphine agreed that this was possibly important and brought her phone over to the computer she kept in her room. By her telling it was hooked up to the same database, which had a record of every angelic person known and suspected, it should, she said, only take a few minutes, especially since Diamond had such a good impression of what the man looked like.

A minute or so later, Mrs. Delphine's eyes widened. Her phone was only facing her, so they couldn't see what she saw.

"Oh no," Mrs. Delphine whispered. "Diamond? Are you sitting down?"

"Why? Is it that bad?"

"I think you should sit down."

What was this—a joke? Everyone looked so serious all of a sudden, like she should listen to what Mrs. Delphine was saying. And...well...fair enough; so she sat down on the couch and held her arms out in expectation.

Mrs. Delphine turned her phone around to face the screen. There was a name—Baraqiel, 'Barry'—and a picture in the top-right corner. There were other stats listed, but the camera wasn't focused enough to make those visible.

"You're *sure* this is the man you saw?" Mrs. Delphine asked.

"That's him. Why, is he—is he dangerous or something?"

"I need you to think hard. Do you remember his face from before tonight? Is there *anything* about him that seems familiar?"

"I told you everything. Who is he?"

Mrs. Delphine sighed. "I'm glad you're sitting down. This isn't going to be easy to take. And I hope there's some part of you that sees this as good news because..."

"Enough with the soap opera suspense. Just tell me—*who is this*?!"

"Oh, Diamond. This is your father."

Chapter 6

It couldn't be. Impossible—no way, nuh-uh, it wasn't him...it couldn't have been! But then there he was, staring right at her—Mrs. Delphine sent over the file to her phone. Diamond sat in the corner of the living room, her knees up to her chin, her phone in her hands...Nobody else said a word. She scrolled from top to bottom, read all his stats, what was known of his biography—she shook her head the whole time, read parts aloud, went back when there were things about which she forgot.

There were rumors about his disappearance, but something prevented Heaven from knowing everything. It all came down to a demonic prince named "Abaddon, the Destroyer"—a libertine, a pleasure-seeking maniac—feared by everyone who knew his name. Diamond mentioned the name to Delphine, and she shushed the girl, her eyes glazed over. Her mind retreated to somewhere else as if even she couldn't take the fear.

Why was everyone so scared of this guy? Abaddon was ancient, they said—he first appeared in the historical record sometime around the Middle Ages, where he was said to bring plague and violence and to attack victorious armies after a battle while they were weak, to take their spoils.

There were paintings of him; tall, with eyes that glowed red in the dark, his gigantic frame towering over everyone. There was even a poem written by a survivor, maybe the one person who came into contact with him and lived, but Diamond had trouble with Middle English and abandoned reading it after three stanzas.

This was the guy who was chasing after her dad. Maybe everyone else was afraid of him, but Diamond wasn't. She put her phone in her pocket, ignoring the exhaustion she felt as the sun came up, ignored Lucas and Marco following behind her, Marco saying, "Where are you going?", and ran off into the chilly morning air.

By the time she reached town, morning was in full bloom, and her inner city girl came bubbling up from her subconscious, only to get pushed away by this determined, angry other self that was taking over an increasing proportion of her mental activity. She wasn't even sure she had a plan—*did* she have a plan? Well, her dad certainly had the look of a homeless guy, which meant he must have been at least hiding amongst them, right? So what did that mean?

At least *one* of the transients had to know who he was. Or have seen him. And she had Barry's—her dad's—picture on her phone, so she could use that.

It wasn't the worst idea she'd ever had, anyway. She caught a cab over to Powderhorn Park and got out right at 14th Ave. S, where right away she came face-to-face with the large homeless encampment that had sprung up over the last few years. Underneath the encampment was one of the most beautiful parks in town, and behind her a small, very Midwestern, blue house surrounded by trees, bushes, and clean lawns.

Right in front of her were three or four—maybe one was a pile of blankets, she couldn't tell—homeless guys sitting on the grass, staring up at the pale sky. She approached them with all the confidence of someone who didn't have a lot of time to waste, took out her phone, and said, "Anybody seen this guy?"

They looked, the three that were awake, and they all shook their heads.

"What about your friend?" She gestured to what may have been a pile of blankets, but she was sure there was a person underneath there.

"He's sleeping," one of them said.

"Yeah? Well wake him up."

The three guys looked at each other funny, then shrugged before one of them leaned over and shook the sleeping guy. It took a few times rocking his body back and forth before the guy woke up, his eyes half closed, looking bothered.

Diamond pushed herself to within a foot or so of him and showed him the picture. The guy blinked, rubbed his eyes—good God he was taking his time! Maybe he needed glasses?

"Well?" she asked, starting to get impatient. "Do you know him or not?"

"There's a fella who lives on the other side of the park," he said. "Goes by the name 'Rambo'. Like the movie. He's the guy you wanna talk to, missy."

"Why? Does he know this man?"

"He just kinda knows everybody. Some of the locals—the ones who live in houses, anyway—they call him "King Hobo". We just call him 'Rambo'."

Alright, that was a start.

She nodded a 'thank-you' and walked deep into the encampment towards where her friend had pointed her. There were eyes on her all the time now, and increasingly so—probably not a lot of people came in here; at least, not a lot of people who didn't *have* to be here.

Some of them laughed, maybe at her, maybe at something else. Some of them were talking to themselves, rolling around the ground, trying to pick up things that weren't there. None of them looked particularly happy, and the tents they'd put up to shelter themselves from the cold were all ready to blow over any second—or they were one hole away from not existing at all.

Towards the far side was a shanty made of plywood and mattresses. A crowd was gathered around one guy, a man with long, crusty hair and a thinning beard who sat in the center in a meditation pose, with his legs folded and his arms across his thighs, his middle fingers pressed into his thumbs. His eyes were closed, and he took in deep breaths.

Diamond slowed down her pace as she approached. The eyes of the men and women in the circle around him all faced her at the same time, which was kind of a creepy, "Children Of The Corn" thing—or

"Village Of The Damned"? She couldn't remember which; it was one of them.

The man in the middle, the one who must have been 'Rambo', spoke: "What do you want?"

"I'm looking for someone."

Rambo smiled. "Information is expensive. What've you got?"

"I can save you money on a hospital bill?"

"I can tell you're joking. Your sense of humor—do you say it's 'dark'?"

"My therapist does. Are you gonna help me or not?"

"Describe him to me."

She stepped into the circle of hobos and handed over her phone. Rambo opened his eyes, took it, and looked at the man for only a second before his face lit up—a reaction he tried to hide almost immediately before giving the phone back.

"Information is expensive," he repeated.

"You recognized him. Don't lie to me."

"So what if I did? I don't have to tell you anything. Not for free."

"Okay. What do you want?"

"Beer."

"I'm not old enough to buy beer. What else?"

"You're not—what do you mean? How old are you?"

"Twenty," Diamond lied.

"Really? Well, you could've fooled me. You look old for your age, and that's not a compliment. Alright, this guy showed up only within the last few days. Calls himself 'Bernard'. But that picture says his name's 'Barry'."

"Yeah," she said. "He's using a fake name. Go on."

"Barry—or 'Bernard', or whatever—said he wasn't staying long, but he needed us to keep our mouths shut about him. I have spies all over town. One of them told me this morning they saw him heading west."

"Okay, but towards where? Edina?"

"That's what he said. Now what are you gonna give me?"

Adrenaline pulsed into Diamond's veins. She said, "I thought you were offering it on the house. Since I can't buy you beer."

The circle of homeless people all stood up at the same time, while Rambo grinned at her from his seated position. This wasn't good—just the optics alone wouldn't do her any favors. She took a step back and held up her hands, said, "I don't have anything," then looked over her shoulder, knowing there was no way she was gonna scrap with homeless people, not least of all when she was outnumbered.

It was human desperation—that's what she reminded herself. This wasn't their fault; they'd been placed here by circumstances beyond their control. Not that that helped her in that moment, with her heart beating so loud she could hear it, her pupils dilating to the point they might stretch out her eyes permanently.

She didn't even have a dollar on her. She didn't have *anything*, much as she wished she did. And behind her was the rest of the encampment, which meant running the risk of bumping into someone who owed Rambo a favor, someone who could jump in at the last second, caught up in this desperation cycle, of owing someone and needing to get out of debt.

In other words, she was completely screwed.

Which was right when a hand landed on her shoulder, scaring the life out of her. She must have jumped four feet in the air, yelped, and then spun around to see a familiar face, one she didn't expect to see—in fact, probably the *last* one she expected to see, given the circumstances.

It was Ty, all smiles as he reached into his pocket, pulled out his wallet, and produced wad of small bills.

"Here," Ty said. "I think this should cover it."

He handed the wad over to Rambo, who snatched it, counted it, and then smiled a big, toothless smile, looking almost like he wanted to throw the bills into the air to see what it felt like to have money rain down on you.

"We're rich!" Rambo exclaimed joyfully enough that he might do one of those stereotypical hillbilly jigs. "Rich!"

Everyone cheered. Everyone except Diamond, who shoved Ty in the chest, knocking him back a step. It wasn't like a dozen hours or so had passed and she'd magically forgotten everything she'd learned about him.

"What are you doing here?" she asked. "Are you following me?"

"Come on," he said. "I've got something I need to tell you."

Chapter 7

Whatever Ty's motives were, they remained a mystery to Diamond, who spent the next—oh, 20 minutes or so—sitting sideways in the passenger seat hugging her knees, resting the back of her head against the window, on the other side of which was the sun setting on Minneapolis and the parking lot in which they sat—and all while Ty's inner self wrestled with whatever tumult was going on inside of him.

Demon—that's what she had to remember; that he was demonic, that he was up to something and likely something terrible. In addition, though, she had to remind herself that he didn't know anything about her yet. He didn't know anything about who she hung out with, who she was, nothing. She had the clear advantage—and she had to keep it that way.

"I have secrets," Ty said suddenly. "There are things about me—ah, forget it. You won't understand."

She didn't say anything. She couldn't give herself away...so she waited.

"I'm not who you think I am," he started again. "There are things I've done that, well...Have *you* done bad things?"

"I'm an alcoholic. I've been to rehab. What do you think?"

"You're an alcoholic?...Never mind. Maybe this was a bad idea."

"How many dates have we been on?"

"Does this one count?"

"No. So, we've been on *three*. Right? You don't have to tell me anything. We're not serious."

"But what if I wanna be serious?"

She had to admit: she didn't expect that. It caught her off guard, and he could tell. He banged his head against the window, but lightly, to tell himself how stupid that was.

"So, now I blew it," he said. "Right? I jumped the shark. I can't help it. I was...you know, I was drawn to you that night. At the club. I don't normally do this, but I feel like I can talk to you. I *wanna* talk to you. And that's not something I've ever done before."

"'*Gun*', by the way. You jumped the *gun*. 'Jumping the shark' means—look, if you wanna *try* being serious—and I don't know if that's, you know... But okay, tell me. I'll listen."

He shuffled in his seat, gritted his teeth...Basically displayed out on his body the back-and-forth that went through his mind, from making wave-motions with his hips, to scratching his arms...Honestly, it was almost adorable, how much he worried about ruining what opinion of him she may have had left over from last time.

There was that moment, last time, where his vulnerability slipped out. Demon or no, there was something in there...

"Do you believe in Hell?" he said. "Like, believing in life after death is one thing, right? But what about *Hell*? Do you think it's real?"

She swallowed. "No."

"I do. I've seen it. Sometimes...I go there when I dream. And I like it."

"Sure, but everyone has bad thoughts."

"My dad says my mom was half angel."

"Your dad," she said, "might be delusional."

"No, no. Because here's the thing—I go to Hell in my dreams because that's where my dad comes from."

She had to feign thinking that that was ridiculous. She went to get out of the car, but he put his hand on her shoulder, just gently, to try and stop her. She let it work, even pretended to listen to him as she let that first thing he said really sink into her brain.

His mom was half angel. That explained this conflict in him; why he wasn't a complete hedonist, a Machiavellian psychopath. Half angel—did that mean there was hope for him yet?

"I wish I could tell you about the things I've seen," he said. "What I've seen him do? I mean, everything from drugs to underground fighting to—"

"That's *nothing*. Some day, I should tell you about what we used to do in the basement of the Cock's Canary. That was crazy..."

"But that's just the tip of the iceberg. Sometimes, I think he gets me to do things for his approval just to see if I'll do them. And I keep...I keep doing them over and over again..."

He clenched one of his hands into a fist, then did the same with his entire body, closed his eyes, and showed his teeth like he was fighting with a memory that wouldn't go away.

Then he said, "He had—you have to listen to me, *he had an angel that he kept locked up in the cellar*."

"He had *what*?" She tried to contain herself—she couldn't help it, but her interest slipped out, and she coughed, breathed, and relaxed. "I mean, isn't that *crazy*? How could he have an angel held captive?"

"Well, that's the thing," Ty said. "I helped the angel escape and now I'm—he's making me help him look for it. He even thinks he knows where it is."

"Where? Or—this is crazy. He's, you know...He needs help, your dad. What if he's hunting down some poor man? What's he gonna do with this guy once he gets a hold of him, anyway?"

"I dunno. He won't tell me."

She took a second. This was crazy. And not just that Ty's father must have been looking for this angel, but—his father *was* Abaddon, wasn't he? And the angel...Unless there was more than one demon hunting an escaped angel, but what were the odds of that?

She had a feeling like she'd been building a puzzle and had a piece that wouldn't fit that just clicked into place. Her heart was going, like, insanely fast, and she wanted to stand up and walk around, get some of this adrenaline out of her system. Except that she couldn't let Ty know what she was feeling. Dammit, she couldn't give herself away...

"I think you should take me home," she finally said.

"You think I'm crazy."

"What I *think*," she said, "is that I need some time *to* think."

"Because you think I'm crazy."

"That's just it—I don't think you're crazy at all."

The person she thought was crazy in this scenario was *her*. As they drove silently back to her place, she ran through what must have been the pros and cons of her plan and only came up with pros. She just needed someone off of whom she could bounce ideas.

Because she was sure that somewhere in there, in her imagination, in this bright idea of what to do next, was the dumbest idea with which she'd ever created.

***

"You're right," Marco said. "That's the dumbest idea you've ever had."

They were sitting out on the porch maybe 20 minutes or so after Ty had dropped her off. The remainder of the drive had been totally silent, which worked out well for her because she'd had time to figure out what she thought were the kinks to the plan, and as far as she could tell, there didn't seem to be any.

Marco, however, thought completely different.

"What's so dumb about it?" she asked. "We have no way of getting a hold of my dad. He's out there being hunted by, apparently, the scariest demon in the whole of reality, and that demon has a bead on him. What could go wrong?"

"Infiltrating the family of the scariest demon known to man. You don't see how that could go wrong?"

"Why are you such a square? You don't think I can take him?"

"I have no idea," Marco said. "And that's kind of the point."

"You can disguise me, right? Don't you have something that can put him off my scent, so he won't detect that I'm an angel?"

Marco gritted his teeth. He wouldn't say so, but it was obvious that he did. And she knew about it because she'd read about those things, so it was a good thing he didn't lie to her.

"So do that," she said. "And he'll never know."

"It's not foolproof!"

"It's worth a shot. This is my dad we're talking about."

Marco leaned against the outside of the house and groaned. The crickets formed a kind of counterpoint to how heated their conversation was getting, like they were the wind of the hurricane and the outdoors was its center.

Of course, the line about her dad would get him. It made him think of his own father, which was the idea—and now he was torn, pacing around, stamping his feet, even *cursing*, which was weird for him.

"Lucas isn't gonna like this," he said. "Delphine? You think you can get her approval?"

"No. Which is why you need to keep quiet."

"Oh no. Come on—"

"Well, what other option do we have? You come up with something; I'm all ears. If we track Ty's family and trace them to my dad, we're letting them stay one step ahead of us. If we try to trace my dad on our own, we're even further behind. Right?"

"I know, I know; will you shut up? I'm trying to think."

"Just give me the magic protection," she said, "and I'll take care of the rest. All you have to do is not tell anybody."

"And what if something happens to you?"

The tone of his voice was, well...unexpected. She was sure she looked like she'd just seen something that didn't make any sense, that her head twitched kinda, and she blinked a lot.

But she must have been reading into it. There was no way Marco felt...

"I'll be fine," she said. "I've been through worse. Believe me."

Marco gritted his teeth again. At this rate, he was gonna grind them down to absolutely nothing, but he quickly groaned and kicked his feet against the ground, making kind of a circle as he must have realized she was right; that this might have been the best option—or, at least, that there was nothing he could do to stop her.

She, of course, really *was* gonna be fine, and she knew that. With that, he took her into his room and showed her how the protection worked.

***

When Ty answered the phone later, it was clear she was the last person from whom he expected to hear. She'd given him the impression, he said, that she thought he was crazy and never wanted to hear from him again.

But the truth, she said, was the opposite. She told him she'd seen the good in him, she was sympathetic to his story—she believed, at least, that Ty's dad was a metaphorical demon, and so she wanted to help. She wanted to meet him.

She did a good job of being the naïve, concerned girlfriend. The one who wants to save her new boyfriend from whatever 'Hell' it was from which he came.

Ty said he didn't think it was a good idea, but she told him how she was getting feelings for him too, which wasn't a lie, really, and how if she saw what he had to deal with then maybe she'd understand.

Eventually, Ty relented. It took some doing, but she got him there.

"I just hope you know what you're getting into," he said. "I'll come pick you up tomorrow."

She hung up and smiled. This was gonna work. She'd save Ty from his father and find her own in the process. There was nothing that could go wrong.

Chapter 8

The mansion stood at the top of a hill, just west of Minneapolis, jagged against the night sky and overlooking a stretch of property so big that it'd take a lifetime to cover every square foot. That lightning struck was no surprise—hell, organ music should have been playing the "Toccata And Fugue", and Vincent Price should have answered the door with his ascot, worn down from burying another wife who'd resurrect right at the moment his sanity was cruelly torn from him by the forces of fate.

Basically, it was gothic, it was Dracula's castle, and she couldn't help but have that inner Bauhaus fangirl grow in curiosity—in excitement—as they approached the circular driveway at the front of the mansion. Even as she got out of the car, her eyes never left it. She looked up at the spires above, the blackened windows that seemed backlit to candlelight.

Or was that just her imagination?

Ty got out of the car and pressed his hand up against her back. It startled her, but she quickly calmed, took a breath, and looked back up at the giant house.

"It's not too late to turn back," Ty said.

"Did you tell him I was coming?"

"He was excited to meet you. He *is* excited."

"I'm sure I can handle it." She smiled at him, and the butterflies crept up in her stomach. He sighed and walked past her towards the door, grabbed hold of the door knocker—

But the door opened before he could use the device, and a man peaked around the opening. He was kind of a stocky fellow with no hair and a snarl that transformed into joy as he recognized Ty, threw the door away from him, and brought the young man into an embrace that lifted his feet off of the ground.

"Master Ty!" he shouted. "I'm so glad to—you've been gone for so long, I never thought we'd see you again."

"How's my dad? Fuming?"

"He misses his boy. And who's this? Wow, a pretty lady...! You never told me you had company."

"I didn't even tell you I was coming. This is Diamond. Diamond, this is Roy. We call him 'Roy Batty'. Kind of a double pun—you know 'Blade Runner'? Plus the, uh...You know, bats. Big gothic mansion?"

"It's very funny," Diamond said, though she didn't feel much amusement. She shook Roy's hand. "Nice to meet you."

"Well, come in," Roy said. "I can't wait to tell Abe his son's come home. And that he brought a pretty girl with him, oh—*he'll be so delighted*!"

'Abe', huh? What was with all the short names?

She smiled and then followed Roy in—well, followed Ty who followed Roy. She didn't wanna appear *too* anxious to get in there. As she stepped in through the door and the mansion opened up, she was faced with a scene that must have been drawn from her fantasy life: a genuine, Roger-Corman-Meets-Tod-Browning interior with a winding staircase that wrapped around to the upstairs, a chandelier that hung in the middle and—unless her eyes deceived her—was decorated with cobwebs. Even the floor seemed so old-country, so *vampiric*, slathered in glamorous designs but with a dusting of—well, *dust*.

She shouldn't be excited, but she couldn't help it. She spun around, taking in the wooden decor, the leather couches and chairs, and the open spaces that led to what must have been a hundred different rooms. Rapture took over when Ty put a hand on her shoulder to snap her out of it.

"You think it sucks, right?" Ty asked, expecting disgust from her. "That I come from money?"

"How could I? It's beautiful. Do you like Vincent Price?"

He was gonna say something when a big, booming voice came from the top of the staircase, a bass-heavy, mean timbre that said "Tyreal," calling him by his first name and echoing throughout the mansion.

Ty gulped—visibly. She'd never seen anyone do that before. But when she followed his gaze to the top of the stairs, her own stomach dropped, and she couldn't help but take a step back and *may* have let out an audible gasp; she wasn't sure.

She'd never seen a man like this before. He was almost like a statue. His shoulders were broad, and his jawline like it really was carved out of stone. His whole frame must have rounded out to seven or so feet tall, but he wasn't lanky. He was big, and as he moved down the stairs, did so with so much grace that she thought there was no way it could have been a real person...

Which, of course, it *wasn't*. It was a thing which carried violence in every step, something that had a goal and a purpose that was absolutely *destructive*. You could see it in how he held himself; she swore it was like he was coiled and could lash out at any second.

'Cruelty'—that was the word. She forced herself not to step back any further as Abaddon—Abe—reached the foot of the staircase and approached his son, who by now had begun shivering, his teeth chattering.

"Where have you been?" Abe asked, not making any attempts to hide his anger. "I've been searching all over for our—you brought her with you?"

"This is my girlfriend, Diamond."

Diamond smiled and extended her hand, but Abe didn't take it. He only smiled at her in a way that sent a chill down her spine—the kind of smile someone gets when they realize they've found a new toy. A smile with no warmth.

She retracted her hand. And then—oh no, Abe took a step towards her. She really had to force herself not to step back, to look strong even as she stared up into his eyes and he loomed over top of her, never losing that cold smile.

"You know," Abe said, "I haven't seen my son in days. And he tells me he's been living at a motel and that he wants me to meet his girlfriend. Why do you think he did that?"

"Because he wants to impress you?"

"Do *you*? Want to impress me, I mean."

"Sure." She swallowed. She understood the impulse. "Every girl wants her boyfriend's dad to like them."

"And if you *weren't* dating my son? Would you want to impress me then?"

She didn't know what to say. She kinda stammered and looked over at Ty, who wasn't looking at her. He was wide-eyed and staring at the ground, while his mind was certainly preoccupied with something else; likely, by the looks of things, trying to keep his fear under control.

"I think you would," Abe said. "I think you'd want to impress me very much. Do you know why?"

"Because you—"

"Because if you don't impress me, I can make you regret it."

Was he—his mouth wasn't moving…? And his face, still adorned with that vicious smile, drew nearer to her as if he was trying to smell her, and finally, she couldn't help herself. She stepped back and couldn't look at him anymore, and he laughed, and Roy joined in while Ty shook his head and looked like he wanted to reach out and rest his hand on the underside of her arm—but didn't.

She tried to smile, too, but she couldn't make it happen. She only wished circumstances were different, that she could really show this 'Abe' what she was capable of; she'd rip him to shreds in an instant without thinking about it.

But then she'd lose the lead she might get on her dad. And she'd certainly lose *Ty*. She had to play it cool, play the girlfriend they all expected. And thank God for the charm that was in her pocket…

Abe slapped her on the back and pointed his other hand straight ahead, towards an archway that led out into a large room and said,

"Roy's made dinner for us. You're both late, which you should never do again, by the way—but we waited because we wanted to see you both. Are you hungry?"

Diamond nodded, said, "Yes," and then followed Abe and Roy through to the dining hall on the other side, which was a wide open room with an extraordinarily tall ceiling, complete with a long table decorated with plates; in all, like something out of a painting.

But that was just it, wasn't it—even though everything looked like a painting, even though it was so glamorous and beautiful, she was seeing it the way a depressive would; as if they'd spent their whole lives looking at a curtain, and the curtain had been drawn to reveal something that was—'grave-like' might have been the right word. 'Sepulchral', if you liked your adjectives on the Latinate side of things.

She scratched at her arms, half-expecting to find herself covered in dirt. She could visualize herself fleeing, turning tail and running right out the front door, going back home and opting for a change of plans. But she didn't need to do that, did she? No, Abe should be the one afraid of *her*, not the other way around.

She took a seat next to Ty while Abe sat at the head of the table. Roy snapped his fingers and a door behind Abe opened; a big, bay door-type thing, and six or seven men, all of whom were exhausted and pale, brought out the meal for them and placed it in front of everyone.

"Don't worry," Abe said to Diamond. "This isn't all. I have something—Roy? Where's the special for our guest?"

"My apologies!" Roy said and bowed to show humility. "I'll have it brought right out."

Diamond's heart sank. That smile had come back to Abe's face, so she said, "You didn't have to—"

"When I heard you were coming, I was so excited. I hope Ty told you."

"He mentioned something about it."

"He's brought girls home before. I hope that doesn't make you jealous. No? Good, because there's nothing to be 'jealous' about. There was one name, oh...'Margaret', I think? She was just as scared of me as you are, but we found out she had her limits."

The doors opened again, and Roy walked out backwards. Two of the cooks were pushing a cart that had—it must have had *something* on it, but it was something Diamond couldn't see because Roy was standing in the way.

"She said she cared about my opinion," Abe began. "And you wanna know what my opinion is? I think soft people are good for one thing and one thing only—the fun I have in making them squirm."

"What's on the cart—"

"Come, come. Stand up."

Abe pushed his chair back and approached her. Why did she get the feeling this whole thing was set up from the beginning? Ty wouldn't look at her. Even as she touched his arm to get his attention, he drew away from her.

And there was a mumbling sound coming from the cart...

Before she could do anything, Abe had her by the arm and pulled her up to her feet. She tried to squirm out of his grasp, but he held on tight; even his grip was like stone. And when he pulled her towards Roy, towards the cart and whatever was on it—something that was squirming itself—her feet dragged across the ground, and she got the sense that this was nothing to him, that he wasn't exerting himself in the slightest.

He threw her onto the ground in front of the cart, and she landed on her knees where the mumbling was louder now. She looked up, gasped, held her hand to her mouth, and stood up, pushing herself back, but landed right in Abe's arms who held her still.

There was a man on the cart. A man who was bound and gagged and trying to say something but couldn't say anything past the towel that had been shoved into his mouth.

"Margaret wouldn't do it," Abe said. "But will you?"

"Do what?"

Something was shoved into her hand. It couldn't have been what she thought it was, but there it was anyway: a whip. She let it drop, but Roy grabbed it again and shoved it into her hand.

"You only have to do—let's say *10* lashes. How's that sound?"

"I can't—"

"That's too bad," Abe said with fake disappointment. "Margaret, you know...She hasn't been seen for a long time..."

Abe stepped back from her, and all at once, the horror of the place became something much worse, something beyond even 'horror'. Because maybe she was wrong, maybe she really was in over her head. Maybe if she fought back now, she'd blow this whole thing. Ty would get hurt, and she'd never find her dad.

But her empathy was off the charts. There was that man, so pathetic in the best sense of that word, completely exposed, terrified.

She had to do it—she couldn't, but she had to force herself. It was only 10. Maybe if this man understood what was at stake here...

"Maybe you need some encouragement," Abe said from behind her, and she turned around to see Abe grab Ty by the top of his head and lift him off the ground, squeezing just enough that the pain was as obvious as that Abe could squeeze harder and make this much, *much* worse.

She could tell by his smile. He was *enjoying* this. She didn't give it a second thought—she faced the man on the cart and mouthed the words "I'm sorry" and brought the whip up, closing her eyes as she brought it down 10 times to the sound of Abe laughing until she dropped the whip and fell to her knees. She gasped, and her eyes grew wet with tears.

What had she done? She couldn't open her eyes for a long time. She could only hear the laughing behind her, Ty yelling at his dad for going too far, that he went *too far*, that he should have gone easy on her.

"But I did," Abe said. "If she'd just open her eyes...?"

She did. Because what could he possibly mean? There was the whip lying across the ground, the cart, exactly where it was before—but what was it that was on top of the cart?

She leapt to her feet and drew near to make sure it was what she thought it was, with no idea how it happened but—was it true? Yes it was; good God it was true! But how—how did this happen...?

A roast pig lay across the top of the cart. One with an apple in its mouth. And across its stomach were a series of symbols that she recognized from having combed grimoires for study, symbols that meant—

"An illusion, alas," Abe said. "At least *one* of us thinks it's funny. And you know, I know you didn't do this for my sake, but it's so nice to finally meet someone my son loves—who can be pushed into doing something they hate."

"This is a joke to you?" she asked.

"Roy? Take her upstairs."

"But wait—"

"Why? I like you. I think I want to keep you around for a bit."

"Keep her around"? In a daze, she let Roy take her to the stairs, to the sound of Ty arguing with his father until she was pushed through a door at the end of a long hallway, the kind that was adorned with portraits that were old enough that they were beginning to rot.

She didn't even get to say anything. Roy shut the door in her face, and she nearly collapsed.

She'd really gotten herself into a load of trouble this time. And the way out didn't seem as clear as it had been earlier.

Chapter 9

It wasn't until later that Ty showed up, sheepishly knocking on her door while she stared out the window at the long expanse of grass and hill that surrounded the mansion. He'd brought her some water, but she wasn't in the mood for simple hydration. Water, she figured, wasn't enough to wash down the guilt she was feeling.

Even if it had all been an illusion, hadn't she been willing to hurt someone in order to—well, wasn't it for everyone's safety? Her own, Ty's...Abe was willing to crush his own son's skull just to make her hurt somebody. 'Cruel' was a word she'd hit upon earlier, and it was the right one. His smile, his laughter—he enjoyed it, didn't he? He enjoyed pushing someone into doing not just something they didn't wanna do, but something that, in doing it, hurt *them*.

And yet that wasn't what she'd been focused on, and it wasn't what she kept coming back to now. She could've turned Abe into one of those splintered logs back at Lucas' place with a single movement; she was sure of it. She'd never been more sure of anything in her life. And where would his smile be then, huh? It'd almost be worth the wait when she'd finally get to do it.

Except that if she'd killed him, she might not ever find her dad. At least this way, there was a chance—but wasn't that awful? Her throat grew thick at the thought of it. She was horrible, terrible...And that was it; it was selfish, and if there had been a real person there and not just that pig carcass...

"You don't want any?" Ty said from behind her.

She'd forgotten he was there. She faced him, his arms wrapped around her, and she smiled at him, then looked over to the glass of water that sat on the nightstand beside her four-poster bed.

"Is he gonna let me out?" she asked.

"It's—you might like it here."

"So I'm trapped."

Ty went to say something but then took it back. He sat down on the bed and held out his arms for her to come to him, but she had no desire. She shook her head, but it was furtive enough she wasn't sure he caught it.

"We never should've come here," Ty said. "I think we should get you out. Tonight."

Her heart skipped. Escape? But if she did...She couldn't. Not now, not with this plan of hers and finally being right about where she wanted.

But what could she say? There was no lie she could use that would make sense, not, "But I like being trapped here!", or, "Maybe it'd be better if we talked your dad out of it?", none of that. Should she tell him the truth? And so what if she *did*? What if she told him who she was, what she was doing here—*who* she was after?

How she wanted to, and could, help him?

She approached him and let her hands rest in his.

"I have to tell you something," she said.

"What do you mean? Can it wait? We have to plan your—"

"No, no. You don't understand. I'm not what you—"

A pounding came at the door. Both of them faced the source of the sound, startled. She even grabbed her chest as he stood up, and the pounding came again, and then again.

From the other side, something like a chuckle barely made it through the door.

"Room service!" the voice called. "You want blanky?"

Another voice followed: "What are you doooooing in there?"

"Oh no," Ty said. Then to Diamond, "These are, uh... You're gonna meet my brothers."

All at once, the door came flying open, and two figures fell over top of one another, collapsed on the ground in a fit of laughter. This wasn't supposed to happen now—and who were these guys, anyway? When did they get here?

They stood up, and Diamond suppressed a gasp. It was in the way they dusted themselves off, the leanness to their bodies, the way they slithered from one position to the next—and, of course, their *eyes*.

"Diamond?" Ty asked. "I'd like you to meet my brothers: Asmodeus and Damballa."

Her hand wouldn't rise to introduce herself. There was always the chance they could smell it on her, smell past the charm she kept in her pocket. She breathed; it had to work, it *had to*.

Both of Ty's brothers were Vipers.

***

The most expensive pizza ever made is the white truffle and edible gold pizza. That it's come down to this, that people *eat* gold, astonished Diamond, and yet, as Roy organized the servants to pass out the dishes for dinner, that was *exactly* what sat in front of her: a white truffle and edible gold pizza.

What exactly was "edible gold"? Since when was gold of any type 'edible'? Was edible gold the same as the gold in Fort Knox? Was there *actually* gold in "Fort Knox", or was that just something she'd thought was true, but never had the opportunity to corroborate?

These questions and many more manifested first after being told what she was eating, and second upon actually seeing the thing. To be honest, it didn't even look that good. But Abe was excited for everyone to eat it, and the two Vipers—they started eating it when it was first handed to them, less like snakes and more like raccoons.

"So," Damballa said to Ty. "Paris, right? We were just in Paris. Ty, you listening?"

"You said—yeah," Ty replied, seemingly emerging from a trance. "I'm listening."

"It was wild. We get off at the airport—it takes soooo long to get to Paris from the airport. It's, like, *way* out of town, and we took a bus.

Somebody told us, you know, 'hey, you didn't have to use that airport, there's another one in town'. Is that true? Does anybody know?"

"Finish the story," Asmodeus said around his pizza.

"Right. So we get there and right away there's this—like we just got off the bus and there's this woman asking for money? Like, for a cause, right? And she's got this little like...What do you call them? Like a 'petition' kinda? She wants us to put our names down, our country of origin, which, you know, 'Hell'? But the thing is she says it's for the handicapped or whatever, but the whole thing's a scam. There's no way this company—European Handicapped Commission or something? It's not real. And the logo was the handicapped parking symbol, I mean come *on*."

"Tell them what we did," Asmodeus chuckled.

"This is great. We told her we had a million bucks we were looking to spend on a charity, right here in Paris. Her eyes lit right up. You should've seen her, dumber than a bag of hammers. We told her to meet us here after eight—right? Wasn't it after eight? No, it must have been later. Yeah, we were—remember, it was still light out at eight? Anyway, we met her after dark, and she was there all excited, and we had this big bag that looked like it was filled with money. And we talked to her, told her how excited we were, really, you know, built ourselves up? Anyway, we put the bag down, and she stood over top of it looking in, practically drooling, when we pulled out this big claw hammer and beat it into her skull."

He laughed hard enough he wheezed and coughed. Asmodeus joined in right at the end, and Abe must have been chuckling from the start, like he knew what was coming and couldn't help himself. Even Ty smiled, or, at least, the demon in him did...

Diamond couldn't. She wouldn't. She gritted her teeth instead, picturing the woman, the scared look on her face—

Damballa slammed his hands down on the table. It was such a sudden change in expression, he must have seen she wasn't laughing and anger took over like a snap of his fingers, and he said, "Why aren't you laughing?"

"It's *funny*!" she insisted. "You hit her with the claw hammer. What'd you do with her after?"

"Do with her—what? Nothing, we just left her there. Hey dad, something's weird about this girl. You know what I mean?"

"Be nice," Abe said. "She's just human."

"Human? No, no. Don't you smell that?"

Her heart seized. Was he serious? Her mouth hung open, and it was apparent something about Damballa saying that triggered a response in everyone in the room, including Ty.

Had Marco's stupid charm stopped working? He'd said it wouldn't last forever, but it shouldn't be over this quickly.

"I didn't shower today," Diamond said.

"Yeah I can smell that, too. What I smell's something different." He pushed his plate aside and leaned towards her. "Who are your parents?"

"A couple of drunks." She smiled. "Rough family."

"Oh yeah? And they're both human?"

"What else would they be?"

"Funny," Damballa said, though he clearly wasn't amused. "Dad, she know what kind of house she's in?"

"I told her," Ty said.

"You've got angel on you," Damballa said. "I'll tell you that right now. I swear to God."

"Don't use that kind of language in this house," Abe warned. "There's only one God. And really—angel? *Her*? Look at her. She's pathetic."

"Thanks," Diamond said, trying not to take offense. "But really, I'm no angel."

"Oh yeah? Prove it."

"How? Seriously, how do you—that's not even possible. You've never heard that you can't prove a negative?"

"What's that mean? Never mind, I've had it."

Damballa got up from his seat and walked around the table towards her. Everyone else was getting antsy, voices were coming from all around her, and Asmodeus' laugh, but nobody, least of all her, was getting up to do *anything* until Ty stood up and pressed his hand into his brother's chest, only for Damballa to toss him out of the way and continue his approach to stand behind Diamond.

He rested his hands on her shoulders. Ty tried to pry him away, but Damballa pushed him off again and—what was she gonna do? Her wings stirred in her back as she visualized the move: pushing the chair out from the table and into his waist to catch him off-guard, then spin around, put a foot up on the chair, leapt and cut his head clean off with the right wing.

That'd just be the first one. From then on, she'd have to—

Damballa leaned in close to her ear. His breath was hot, disgusting, and she closed her eyes as he said, "I can smell you," and then—

He licked her face and laughed.

"Got you!" he exclaimed. "You guys fell for it!"

She exhaled. Ty said something like, "That's not funny,", and Damballa just laughed some more and then went around the table back to his seat where he continued eating his gold pizza.

It was so stupid. It was all so *stupid*. And the gold pizza didn't even taste that good, and all they talked about was the people they'd hurt, and the terrible things they'd done, and every second was an eternity in this place; every minute torturous beyond expression.

When she was finally done, she thought about excusing herself early, but there was no way Abe would go for that. So, she waited for everyone to be finished, until the table was cleared, and Abe got up and said he'd be in the living room. Everyone said goodbye to him, and Diamond pushed her chair back, intending to go back upstairs, to wait until something came up with her dad.

But as she approached the stairs, a hand grabbed hold of her arm from behind her. It was Damballa, with a look unlike the one he'd had on earlier—this was him deadly serious.

"Where are you going?" Damballa asked.

"Not with you, but thanks for asking."

"Funny. Listen—I'm keeping an eye on you. You hear me?"

"Good, because I'm very, *very* dangerous. Do you mind?"

She tried to pull away, but he squeezed harder. He was strong. But if she felt like it—

"The charm," Damballa said. "The one in your pocket? It's wearing off."

He let her go, and she ran up the stairs.

Chapter 10

Abe couldn't tell yet, and that was the important thing. Damballa must have been biding his time, waiting for the right moment—when it would be so clear to him, so obvious, that there was no chance of getting on his dad's bad side as a result. Like, if he made the wrong call—if she wasn't an angel—and then ruined Abe's plans for her, whatever those might be, the punishment he could receive...well, it could be severe, if the rest of Abe's behavior was any indication.

Okay, so where did that leave her? She paced around her room with increasing speed, kinda mumbling to herself and thinking—if the charm was wearing off this quickly, she'd just have to get it, like, reupped or whatever, right? And as much as Abe thought she was trapped, as far as she was concerned, she was letting him keep her here, so she might as well—

What, escape? Okay, but how?

A breeze came in—it was from the window, which she'd left open just a crack. The curtains billowed. It was that easy, eh? All it took was peering out the bedroom door into the hallway, listening for footsteps and hearing none, then she closed the door as gently as she could, took a running start and leapt from the window.

Her wings came out instantly and straightened right before she was gonna hit the ground, pulling her upward and into the air. It was warm that night, maybe the last warm night for a while. She closed her eyes and breathed because everything was gonna be fine. She was getting out of this. She was gonna find her dad, beat the bad guy, everything. And it was gonna be *easy*.

She landed in front of Lucas' house and threw open the front door as quickly as possible, then slid in through the kitchen looking for Marco. Video game sounds came from the living room, so she ran over there and leaned in to find Marco sitting on the couch with a controller in his lap. He didn't even notice she was there, so she coughed and startled him.

"Where have you—"

"I need your help," she said, cutting him off. "The charm's starting to run out on me. I almost got caught."

"Okay, but you've been gone for longer than I'd thought—"

"I know, and I don't have time to explain everything! Can you help or not?"

Marco set the controller down and held out his hand. She placed the dream catcher-looking object in his hand, and he said "Give me sec," then went down into the basement. Sounds of rummaging around came up and through the cellar door while she tapped her foot, hopelessly aware of how much time was passing.

Jeez, how long was this gonna take, anyway? What if someone back there was looking for her? What would she say—that she went for a walk? Maybe this was a bad idea, but the charm, obviously, she really did have to do something about that...

Marco came back up a few minutes later, exasperated, like he couldn't believe he was doing this again. He placed the charm in her hand, but paused a moment. And what was that on his face—confusion? He wanted to tell her something, and finally, he said, "I really hope you're being safe."

"Are you kidding?" she laughed. "I'm basically letting him keep me there."

"You know, I've seen this 'attitude' in you, or whatever you wanna call it...I've seen it grow. Ever since Night Adder. Aren't you worried you're putting yourself at a disadvantage?"

"Are you saying I'm being too cocky? You don't think I can take Abaddon?"

"I think you can do anything."

There was something about his tone. It kindled something inside her, some burning sensation that caused her mouth to open and a sharp, deep breath to fill her lungs.

And what was that sound? Rain tapped against the windows. Marco grabbed hold of her hand and held it tight, and the rain came down harder, drowning the silence outside. She couldn't help herself. She squeezed his hand back and allowed herself to be pulled towards him with a gentle tug as his free hand found its way around her back.

"What are we doing?" she asked, knowing *exactly* where they were heading.

"I don't know. I just—do we have to 'talk'?"

She shook her head. And all at once, it was like something outside of her propelled her towards him, closed her eyes in time with his, and brought their lips together.

***

She sat at the edge of the bed with her head in her hands. Marco slept on the other side. The rain had stopped. The thunder had been loud, and the lightning bright. The storm had enveloped them both.

From where had all these feelings come? They'd first appeared when she'd met him but hadn't they subsided? Hadn't they gone away? And what was she feeling now, but absolute ecstasy once her fingertips touched his back, the hammering of her heart against her breastplate? She retracted her hand and put her head again in her hands, pulling down on her cheeks while taking in a deep breath through her nose.

She had to get moving. Should she say goodbye to him? Of course not, she'd be back; she'd see him in no time. She got up, dressed, and went out the front door before taking to the skies, this time into the cold night air that pricked against her cheeks and settled in her eyes like hard ice.

She went in through her window with as close to silence as she could. Her feet seemed to barely touch the ground they were so quiet, and she turned and closed the window, when—

"I knew it."

She jumped, spinning around quickly. The room was pure darkness, but there was a shadow in the far corner, a morphological monstrosity of blackness that shifted as she tried to figure out what the hell that thing was.

She backed into the wall, made a fist with her right hand, and steeled herself up.

"Who's there?" she asked.

"Don't you recognize my voice? Maybe I should come into the light..."

The lights came on quickly. Her eyes recoiled. She turned her head and blinked until they adjusted, then faced the corner, her palms slick as a bead of sweat fell down the side of her face.

Damballa and Asmodeus were in the corner. Damballa in front, smiling, rubbing his hands together. His sycophantic brother hid behind him, laughing but in a much more weaselly tone.

"I knew I'd catch you," Damballa said. "It was your smell. You know what half-breeds smell like? Kinda like garbage."

"You're making a huge mistake."

"I've heard this before. You know, one time there was a half-breed—I think her name was 'Michelle'? She had that whole 'bad attitude' thing you've got, like she thought she was *real* tough. She'd been living on the streets for years until she got picked up by some family—and that's where I found her—"

"I'm a bit old for story time; you wanna speed this up?"

"I'm saying I killed her."

"And that's the end of the story?" Diamond asked. "I already figured that out. What's your point?"

"My point—she thought she was tough but she wasn't!"

"Okay, well *I* am tough. Do you know how many Vipers I've killed? Remember Night Adder?"

Damballa scoffed. "Liar, liar! You didn't kill Night Adder, he was killed by—wait a minute..."

"News travels slow around here, huh?"

"It *was* you, wasn't it? Hear that Asmodeus? We're gonna kill the piece of garbage that took Night Adder!"

This was getting ridiculous. Asmodeus was laughing like a kid who'd just come down the stairs at Christmas and that stupid grin Damballa wore didn't make him look half as menacing as he thought. Really, she couldn't help it; she rolled her eyes and said, "Who wants to try first?", but they weren't listening, or they didn't care, because both of them rushed her at the same time.

It was just like she practiced—she got into a lunge position, then pushed off with her forward foot, tucked herself in, and spun as she let her wings fly out, imagining this was just in the cellar with the logs. Except that now it was two Vipers that her wings ripped up, killing them both before she landed on her feet.

See? It was easy. Actually, it was even easier than she'd imagined. The only trick now was to—

A knock came at the door. The two Vipers were splayed out in front of her in a heap, and someone was banging on the door, again and again, with increasing impatience.

"Hold on a second!" she called.

"You have to come now," Ty said from the other side. "I wanna show you something."

"I'm not dressed."

There was a pause before he said, "Can I—"

"What? No. Just hold on."

This was a development she hadn't considered. She thought about showing him what she'd done, but what if he didn't understand? He'd have to, because this was all a part of getting him out of here, of liberating him from the demonic.

But if he didn't, she was gonna blow everything. Fortunately, there was *just* enough space underneath her bed to shove the bodies, at least as a place to keep them for now. So she got down on her knees, pressed her shoulder into the bodies, and pushed.

"What's going on in there?" Ty asked.

"It's nothing. Girl stuff. Can you be patient please?"

"Are you sure you don't need any help?"

"We're not there yet," she reminded him and pushed one last time so that the bodies were under the bed. Then, she took a step back and looked. As far as she could tell, they were hidden perfectly.

She just needed to change her shirt to hide the blood. She peeled her T-shirt off, grabbed a fresh one from the closet, and then rushed to the door, pasting on the best smile she could.

"Follow me," Ty said, but he paused and looked her up and down, brow furrowed. "All that just to change your shirt?"

Well, what could she do but laugh and shrug before she followed him?

***

There was a long staircase that led down into the basement. To Diamond's mind, it was kinda like the Batcave—it got colder as they went deeper down through the basement and finally into the sub-basement, where the sound of computers overworking filled the air, and Abe, finally visible as Diamond rounded the corner and the room opened up to her, sat at a large collection of monitors, frantically typing away at a keyboard.

It really *was* like the Batcave. There were things down here, almost like Abe had been taking souvenirs from time, things she'd never thought she'd see, like the long rows of huge glass cases filled with manuscripts and which had a plaque at the front, on a stand.

What was it? She was drawn to it, the plaque written in Greek which said 'Αλεξάνδρεια', and her breath was sucked out of her.

"Is this—" she began, but Ty shushed her and waved over to the display monitors. Could Abe have plundered the Library of Alexandria before it was burned to the ground? What kinds of books would he have in there...?

And what was that thing at the far end—the circular object surrounded by machinery, like a porthole, the one that made the ominous whirring sound...the sound that burrowed into her brain?

Ty grabbed hold of her wrist to stop her about three feet or so behind Abe, who, after a minute, leapt up to his feet and said, "I found you! You miserable little—you wretch! You maggot! I found you!"

"I wanted to show you this," Ty said in a whisper. "I'd had some people following him. They texted dad with the location, and dad patched into the CCTV network. He's come back into town."

But who? She peered over Abe's shoulder and looked around at the monitors, one on which had a couple arguing, another on which had a woman walking her dog.

The one in the far corner, that was the one at which they were looking. She knew it. Because she'd recognize that face anywhere.

It was the face of her father.

Chapter 11

She couldn't catch her breath. Abe must have thought he was torturing her by bringing her along, but he had no idea what he was getting himself into by doing so. He bragged and boasted about how she was "gonna see me kill something holy tonight", but that wasn't gonna happen—she was gonna steal him right out from underneath that demon bastard.

That was why she let Abe drag her along, deep into the heart of Minneapolis, right downtown where the tall buildings sheltered the moon and the air grew colder and colder. She shivered, but maybe it was excitement? Hard to tell. Ty stood close by as if he was ready to defend her at the slightest provocation. It was sweet, that defensive look he wore about him, but what if she'd told him about who she was, when she'd wanted to? Would he still feel the same way...that he needed to protect her?

Would she even be here now? Or how deep did Ty's love for his father go?

They stood outside a 24-hour cafe, and Abe stopped, put his hands behind his back, and lifted his arms to stretch his chest. It was a false motion—he didn't have to stretch his chest at all—but it was a comical one, and he looked at Ty from out of the corner of his eye as if to wink. Ty didn't see him, his fingers were twitching as he wanted to—she guessed—reach out and grab her hand.

"He's inside," Abe said. "Ty, you know he's gonna be—"

"He's gonna be tough. I know."

She couldn't blame Ty for what he was doing. His dad had him under a spell, what with the threat of death and violence otherwise hanging over him. And Ty didn't know what Diamond's connection to Barry was, so how could she blame him?

Plus, when Abe had gone looking for the two Vipers, his sons, he'd gone into a rage after he couldn't find them. He'd thrown things all over the house, smashed things...It had spooked even her for a bit, so what would Ty feel in that moment? How could Ty ever stand up to his dad and tell him that he couldn't do...well, *anything*?

"You owe me for this," Abe said. "Remember. You're the one who let him go. And if he gets away again..."

Abe cracked his knuckles. There it was. There was everything Ty feared in one motion. Ty even closed his eyes just before Abe took a step up in front of the door, opened it, and walked inside, with Ty behind and Diamond in the rear.

Inside was bright. Everything had kind of a yellow or brown color, and there was the counter with the glass case that displayed pastries and other confectioneries, followed by a layout of tables and chairs, most of which were empty except for two, hooded homeless men sitting in the far corner.

This was it. Abe looked at them and a half-smile crawled up his face. His body was ready to pounce, and at that moment, it was clear he didn't care if he grabbed and killed the wrong one; he'd tear the wrong one to pieces and then get a hold of Barry—

Something buzzed.

The three of them looked around for a second, and one of the two homeless men's head twitched like he wanted to look up but couldn't quite yet. What was it? It buzzed again, and Abe groaned, stepped aside, and answered his cell phone.

"What do you want?" Abe snarled. "You know I'm—no. No, no. Really."

Alright—something had *clearly* gone wrong here. Diamond shook, and Ty caught the expression on her face, stepped towards her, and went to put a hand on her except that he couldn't take his eyes off his dad, who Diamond was sure, even though he was standing behind her, was staring at her.

Abe hung up his phone and exhaled like a bull.

"It's your brothers," Abe said to Ty, and she didn't need to hear the rest of it. It must have been Roy who called. He must have found the bodies under the bed.

She didn't have any longer than a couple seconds to make a decision. One of the homeless men finally looked up and saw the three of them. He stood up and took his hood down to reveal, yes, it was Barry. He was afraid, but Diamond couldn't let him get away, not now that everything was blown.

"Run!" she yelled and got down into a lunge, pushed forward into her heel, and spun through the air. She threw out her wings and corkscrewed towards Abe, seeing ahead at the evisceration that was coming—

Only for Abe to grab hold of her leg, right above the ankle, and slam her into the ground.

She'd never felt anything like it. Every square inch of her body hurt. Her head spun and her vision blurred and swirled, kinda like in a bad acid trip. She knew she was drooling, but there was nothing she could do to stop it. And the voices. The low-pitched and indecipherable voices...

"How long have you known?" Abe shouted. "Answer me!"

"I didn't—"

She pushed herself up into a kind of half-plank pose and shook her head. Everything was coming back into focus now; the shapes in front of her, all three of them—Jesus, Abe had Barry by the back of the neck. Barry was squirming, trying to get away.

Ty was—it didn't matter what Ty was doing. Diamond groaned, clutched the ground, and forced herself up to her feet. She dove forward, towards the shape that she was sure was Barry, tackled him at the waist and fell to the ground, both of them a few feet away from Abe, who'd been caught off-guard and lost his grip on the angel.

They had only a second to get out of there. Barry must have known by now she was there to help, because he pulled her up and took her towards the back exit while Abe's footsteps drew closer. If only she could get her sight back...

"We've gotta move," Barry said. "Do you know how stupid you are?"

"You're welcome," she replied just as they stepped out into the city. Barry's wings shot out from his back and got into position to fly them into the air, only for Abe to come barreling through the exit, wrecking the door's perimeter and splintering it into a thousand pieces. He was winding up for a punch that landed square into Diamond's shoulder and sent her and Barry hurtling into the building next to them.

Barry's body cushioned her—she didn't think she'd have had a chance if he hadn't hit the building first. And all at once, Abe came towards them again, as the darkness of the street they were on seemed to go on forever, as though there really was *no way out*, that they were dealing with an unstoppable beast.

But nothing was 'unstoppable', was it? She yelled as loud as she could, spread her wings, and ran towards Abe, meeting halfway on the street and using their razor-sharp edges to try and tear through his chest, expecting a spray of blood and a scream of pain but only getting from him a chuckle as the wings seemed only to graze him and left not even a single mark.

That wasn't supposed to happen. She could take him, she knew she could—she just had to try again, so she dodged his hand as he tried to grab her, then pushed herself up into a vertical leap so that her shoulder would collide with his jaw.

Something in her arm snapped. She felt the joint dislocate, and she tumbled backwards, fell over onto her back, and pushed herself away from Abe with her heels.

This was why everyone was so afraid of him. He was amused by her; it was almost as if he hoped this would go on, that he could toy with her. Good God, she'd made a mistake...

"Stop!" came a voice from behind him. "Please, stop!"

It was Ty. He was standing at the opposite end of the street, breathing hard, slumped forward with his arms out. Abe looked at him for only a second, just long enough for he and Diamond to figure out at the same time that it wasn't Abe to whom Ty was talking.

"Is this real?" Ty asked, his voice filled with disbelief. "You lied to me?!"

She wanted to answer—really, she did. But something grabbed her by the good shoulder and before she knew it, she was up in the air.

***

Diamond didn't know how much time had passed before Barry dropped her off in the woods. She'd been thinking too much, seeing Ty's expression on repeat. Of course she'd lied to him. She'd lied because she thought she could save both him *and* her father. And now, with the way everything had gone, what were the chances something bad happened to Ty?

But she didn't have time to think about that now. Barry was standing over top of her, feeling around her shoulder when he pressed it inwards with a quick motion that popped it back into place.

"There," Barry said. "Now you'll have to tell me just what the hell you're doing. Aren't you the one who ran me over?"

"Depends on how ready you are for a bombshell."

"Try me."

Diamond got more comfortable—actually, she laid down and looked up at the stars before she closed her eyes and said, "I'm your daughter."

"Daughter? That's—oh my God. Your mom—"

"Yeah. Helen. Remember her? Well, meet your progeny, big guy."

Now it was Barry's turn to sit down. She could tell without opening her eyes that he was in shock, that he wasn't sure if he should smile or just what the hell he should do.

She was kinda glad he opted to not do anything but sit quietly for a few moments.

"How'd you fool them?" he asked.

And at that moment, she told him everything. How she was in love with the half-demon son of Abaddon, her plan to save everyone, and how she'd had to kill two Vipers and that was what led to her discovery. To his credit, Barry listened intently. In a certain sense, she hadn't expected that.

"It was a stupid plan," Barry said. "But at least part of it worked. The only question now is for how long?"

"I thought I could kill him. He's stronger than I thought."

"And you haven't seen the half of it. Listen, I don't want you to think I'm not grateful. But if you've told me everything you know, then you don't know *squat*."

"What do you mean? You were held captive, Ty helped you escape, and now he wants you back. Now I have you, so we figure out a way to get rid of him, and you're home free."

"This is waaaay deeper than that. And not just deeper, but much worse. You're talking about a demon who has a direct connection with the Dark Ones, and they're getting him to move the pieces into place to make a really, *really* big move."

The tone of his voice—jeez, he really meant all this, didn't he? It wasn't just Abaddon that Barry was scared of; it was something else, something much more primal. It was in the shivering of his voice, the shakiness in the rest of his body.

And it was contagious. By now, her eyes were wide open and without even trying to, she was sitting up straight, staring her father right in the eyes, not blinking, not moving a muscle.

"I don't get it," she said. "What 'big move' are you talking about here?"

"He doesn't just want me. He *needs* me. Because the Dark Ones are gonna use me to start the end of the world."

Chapter 12

This time, when she went into the house, it was *Lucas* who was inside, and who spun around from standing over the stove. A surprised look grew on his face before he started stammering and looking around the kitchen for a chair he could pull out and which Barry could sit on.

Barry did that for himself, however. He sat down and leaned his head back, groaning.

"We can't stay here," Barry said.

"Are you—" Lucas started to say, but cut himself off, turned off the stove, and grabbed the chair next to Barry. "You're *him*, right?"

"You said Ty knows where you live," Barry said to Diamond, ignoring Lucas in the process. "So we need to find somewhere else to be."

"I'm just gonna grab my things," Diamond said. "Two seconds."

Barry's impatience became more pronounced, so Diamond hurried upstairs and into her room, where she grabbed a suitcase and threw in as many of her things as she could. From behind her, the door opened and a light rapping came. For the first time, she rolled her eyes at what must have been her father's impatience, and which made her feel—kinda good? That was unexpected, but being the daughter of an annoying father felt reassuring...*normal*, even...

Until the voice she heard wasn't her father's: "Where are you going?"

She froze. She didn't know why—she'd known Marco for a long time and what had happened between them...She didn't wanna talk about it, even if something about his voice said that was exactly what he was looking to do.

"I have to leave," she replied. "You should, too."

"Are they coming for you?"

She was surprised to see the worry and sadness in his eyes. It was almost like he wanted to hold her, but was that what *she* wanted? She must have been looking at him funny. She could tell by his expression; the shock, the fear, the unease.

She took a step towards him, but couldn't lift her eyes from the ground once she did. His hand raised and one of his fingers crooked in her direction.

"I knew you couldn't stay," he admitted. "But I wanted you to. The other night, I mean."

"We don't have time for this." She tried to sound impatient, but her voice was soft. "You need to grab your things and get as far away from here as you can."

"What if I wanna go with you?"

"You don't. It's only gonna be more dangerous."

"I think I know better than anyone what I want."

She pressed her thumb and forefinger on either side of his outstretched hand. If he knew half of what she'd seen, he wouldn't wanna be anywhere *near* her. But then...why couldn't she tell him? Was it because she wanted him to come with her, too?

What if—was it so stupid to think that maybe Marco was safer with her and Barry? Wasn't he more exposed if he was off on his own? Maybe not if he went to the Reservation, but—maybe if there were three of them, they'd have a better chance of ending this as quickly as possible.

"You shouldn't come," she said. "This guy is—he's dangerous. *Beyond* dangerous. I couldn't handle him."

"I've already made up my mind. I'm going with you."

All she could do was nod. It was what he wanted, no matter what she said. She finished packing and ran downstairs to grab her dad.

***

Lucas had just gotten the car fixed, so he wasn't keen on parting with it again. But once they dropped him off at the facility with Mrs. Delphine, he was safer than any of them because he was separated from everybody else. Abaddon was gonna be looking for them, without a doubt. They had a very small window of time, but they needed to find some place to hole up where they could think and come up with a plan.

There was a motel headed towards Wayzata—it was a long drive, but the distance wasn't gonna hurt them. They drove in dead silence the whole way; Marco in the driver's seat and Diamond in the back, until they reached the spot: a seedy little Motel 6. Quietly, they checked into two rooms and holed up in the one in which Diamond and Marco were gonna sleep.

It smelled in there. Like cigarettes. And the heat was working overtime. It was a loud thing coming from somewhere. Even the chair over by the corner table should have been thrown out years ago; it sagged under Diamond's weight, and she wasn't exactly 'big'.

For a few moments, they all sat staring at each other; Marco leaning up against the wall and Barry sitting on the bed with his elbows on his knees. Did nobody wanna say anything? Was *that* the problem?

"Where do we start?" Marco asked.

"We need to kill him." Diamond looked to her dad. "Right?"

Barry shrugged. "Ideally. But who knows if that's even possible? Diamond, you saw his sub-basement, didn't you?"

"Sure. It's where he gets access to all the CCTV cameras and things like that."

"Did you see kind of a circular thing—got machines all around it?"

"Yeah. Yeah, sure, I saw that."

"That's a portal. Like, to the other world. You understand? That's why Ty let me go; because if Abe opens it—and he can only open it with the blood of an angel—then the whole of Hell comes marching out of it."

"And that's the end of the world," Diamond finished for him. "Right?"

"Unless you guys happen to know a Medicine Man."

"We do," Marco said. "My brother. He's safe."

"Good. Listen, for whatever reason, the Dark Ones have seen fit to move the time frame up. I'm not sure why. I don't even know if *they* know. But this wasn't supposed to happen yet."

"We can use Ty again," Diamond said.

Marco shook his head, but Diamond cut him off, saying, "This isn't the time for jealousy."

"Forget jealousy," Barry said. "We're not using the daddy's boy. No, come on—hey, listen, which one of us do you think knows him better?"

"Maybe I've seen something you haven't."

"He let me go. I know there's some good in him. But he wants his daddy's approval more than he wants anything else most of the time. It's not a chance we can take."

That was wrong. She knew it—but why bother saying anything? She only sighed and put her head in her hands. "Then what's the plan?"

"We run. We hide. There's no stopping him."

"That's impossible," Marco said. "There has to be some kind of combined power we have, something—"

"What'd I tell you?" Barry's voice was growing harsher. Fear crept into it. "I've been around this guy long enough I know *all* his secrets. I know all the devious, evil things he's done, and most of them aren't anything I'd bother repeating. Diamond, you fought him—you know. There's nothing you can do to beat him."

"Then what does that do for the war, huh? Do we lose?"

"The Medicine Man chooses. You know that already. But other than that, yes. The end of the world is coming, and there's nothing you, nor I, nor anybody else can do to stop it."

In a way, she was surprised by her dad's cynicism. Maybe it was that he was an angel—yeah, maybe, *maybe* because angel's were supposed to be righteous and good, and Abe had beaten him down so much that he was a hollow shell of a man.

But it was obviously not true. This could be prevented, it could be put off. She shook her head almost violently and said, "You must have seen something. *Anything* that looks like a weakness."

"You wanna know how I first met him?" Barry asked. "Fine—I'll tell you."

***

"Your mother and I first met when your mom was an administrative aide to the Secretary-General of the UN. From what she told me, she'd worked her entire life towards this, and she was more sure than she'd ever been sure of anything that she was gonna have a long career in politics.

Her big job was helping him as he tried to quell a genocide in—you know, I can't remember. It's been a long time. Somewhere, anyway. But this kinda fulfilled that promise she'd made to herself as a young woman that she'd get involved in something that mattered, you follow? She was idealistic, as all young people are.

And frankly, so was I. Even made the dumb request to be sent down to Earth because, contrary to popular belief, angels don't just sit around pruning their wings. We get things *done*; we work hard to keep things in check. And there was a rumor about a terrorist attack taking place in the middle of this genocide, which of course would make everything about a gazillion times worse, and I had the bright idea I could get in the middle of the whole thing and stop it.

Once I got there, it was clear that somebody was funding this terrorist operation. I looked into it and eventually caught word of some guy named 'Abe' who wasn't putting money in this for any reason—not that anyone could tell, anyway. In fact, if anything, it looked like the guy wanted to do it for nothing other than the pleasure he'd get from making matters worse.

This was how I met your mother. She'd overheard the Secretary-General mention something, having a conversation with somebody...Her and I—we fell in love, which happens sometimes, you know, between angels and people. We were together on this because she was brave and, yes, *idealistic*, at least until we found out it was the Secretary-General who was taking bribes and helping fund the operation.

We tried to stop it. We *really* did. Abe got a hold of your mother and tortured her until she gave up my location. I got swarmed later. I thought I was coming home to her, but instead I found Abe, and he beat me and took me away.

Your mother lost her job, obviously. Abe was sure to tell me that her life was ruined, that she'd never work in politics again. And I haven't seen her since. That was 20 or more years ago, and since that time, I've never seen Abe do anything that benefited anyone under *any* circumstances. This is the man who planned to make a genocide worse just because he thought it was amusing."

***

"I never found out what happened to her," Barry finished.

"Well, she's doing great," Diamond said. "Even picked up a drinking problem to celebrate all her successes."

"I didn't even know she was pregnant. I didn't...Well, I didn't even get to tell her who I was. And now we're screwed. Hell, short of bringing in the Angel of Death himself, there's nothing we can do to stop Abaddon."

Diamond looked at Marco, who was already looking at her.

"What'd you say?" Marco asked.

"I said—wait. No, no, don't even think about it."

"What about the Angel of Death?" Diamond asked, her curiosity peaking. "Can we actually do that?"

"That's the dumbest idea you've ever had. Believe me."

"Why? Does he not do requests?"

"He does, there's just a—do you not know what the cost is? Of bringing in Azrael?"

"What do you think?" Diamond asked. "That we're asking all these questions because we're experts?"

"He doesn't just *do* requests. No. If you want Azrael to take a life, you have to offer a life up in addition to the one for which you're asking. You have to make a sacrifice."

"Our own life?" Marco asked.

"It's something you can't live without, so, yeah. Usually."

"Okay," Diamond said, "then I'll offer up—I dunno, I have a Bauhaus record that's pretty rare—"

"You think the Angel of Death cares about *Bauhaus*? I'm just saying, if we're gonna do this, one of us is gonna have to go up with him. Taking a life isn't something he takes lightly; he demands *sacrifice*."

She was sure she could do something to change Azrael's mind, sure that the Angel of Death would see how important this was and do something to help them. This was an angelic being they were talking about, not one prone to selfishness, or—at least, her dad notwithstanding.

No, she didn't believe the Angel of Death wouldn't see through to helping them. And if it was gonna take some convincing, she was sure she could do something about it.

"Alright," Diamond said. "Tell me how we get in touch with the Angel of Death."

Chapter 13

Barry explained everything, but only to convince her to back down. To begin with, they had to get close enough to whomever it was they wanted the Angel of Death to take that they could physically offer up the life to Azrael, which was then followed with a prayer that was, in all fairness, simple enough to memorize. Secondly, Azrael had to agree that this was the right call, which probably wouldn't be the difficult part. But then they had to offer a sacrifice, which was where things would get dicey. So, altogether, they had to get close enough to Abe without him killing them first, then sacrifice something.

She had to admit: it did sound impossible. And the more she tried to find a way around this set of rules, the more roadblocks her dad put up to it until she got frustrated and walked out the front door to get some air.

Did she bother to close the door? She didn't remember. She was clutching the railing that made up the little porch in front of the motel room and staring right into the ground, knowing there had to be a way around all this.

She didn't even notice the hand on her back. Marco came into view gradually, growing into her peripherals until he stood next to her, exhaled through his nostrils, and wiped his sweaty palms onto his pants.

"There's another way," he said. "I'm sure of it."

"Is there? Well if you figure out what it is—"

He recoiled from her tone. She couldn't blame him. She groaned at her inability to keep her temper down and said, "I'm sorry. I just can't figure out—is there *nothing* simple in the world? You know what I mean? Like, there's no way we just kinda waltz in there, whoop his ass, and get out scot-free? And now you're involved, so I'm dragging you into this crap..."

"I don't mind. *Really*. Plus, I can't stand the thought of you doing this alone."

What did he mean? She threw him a puzzled look as his eyes shifted between her and the ground; his right hand, the one closest to her, tapped against the railing.

"You're talking about the other night," she said.

"Well? I mean, I've always thought, you know...Is that weird? I'm sorry, I don't wanna make things awkward—"

"'Awkward' isn't the right word. It's just your timing, right now, sucks."

"I know. I just don't wanna wait too long."

Too long for what? The inside of her head was spinning—for the love of God, why did he have to bring this up *now*? She wanted to press herself into him but instead rested her head on his shoulder and closed her eyes. His breathing became sharper, and his hand rested on hers as her own breathing became sharp in time with his. Without the benefit of sight, they swirled together, connected at the hand; connected from her ear to his arm, their breaths in unison and in time with the single, unified, beating of their shared heart.

It really *was* a nice night. And it was nice having him next to her, for what it was worth. She just hoped he knew that.

She was even gonna tell him when the wind came at her kinda funny and blew her hair into her mouth. She pulled the strands away and—from where was this weird feeling coming?

"You feel that?" she asked.

Marco shook his head. "I don't think so?"

Maybe she was going crazy. But she didn't think so. There was litter around the parking lot that should have been blowing with that gust of wind, but it was all perfectly still—old fast food wrappers, an empty pack of cigarettes, and more.

This wasn't right. She could sense it. Marco wasn't quite the empath she was, so maybe whatever this was escaped him. Like how, back into the motel room, her dad was standing straight, his leg in mid-stride...Mid-stride, eh? Marco wasn't moving, either. There was even condensed breath coming out of his mouth that rested in the air.

Had someone...stopped time?

Whoever it was, they were looking at her. Their eyes bore into her, but they weren't beside her, not on either side, but right across the parking lot, visible suddenly like they'd snapped into focus, wearing a hoodie, with their head down—a masculine shape, but one she'd recognize anywhere.

"How'd you find me?" she asked.

Ty smiled and began a slow approach. "We have eyes everywhere. Far cry from that farmhouse you were at before, isn't it?"

"If you've come here to fight—"

"Is this your new boyfriend?"

She steeled herself up. This wasn't fair. She didn't wanna do this, not now.

"How many lies have you told me, then?" he asked. "For sure about you being a half-blood. About you having another boyfriend, by the looks of it, which is a lie by omission if I've ever seen one. What about your reason for staying with me? At my family home? Was it only to save this, uh—who's this angel, anyway? Your dad?"

"It wasn't to get kidnapped, I'll tell you that."

"I didn't do that. And I tried to warn you."

"Okay. Fine. I wanted to save my dad. But you don't have to live like you do either, you deserve—look, I know you're here to take my dad away so you can impress your own. How's that?"

Ty stopped. He was about three feet from the railing now, his hands jammed into his pockets. Through the darkness, his pearly smile was visible, and he laughed at her like he'd smash something if he didn't.

"You're right," he said. "I did come here to take the angel back."

"That's not happening."

He smiled and pulled something out of his pocket that he set on the railing between them. It was clearly a charm—and she guessed already what it was used for but he told her anyway.

"Once this thing breaks," Ty said, "time's gonna start again. And then you're welcome to try and stop me."

He wasn't thinking rationally. He was heartbroken. She didn't wanna do this, but he wasn't giving her much choice. Every muscle in her body tensed all at the same time. A scream came from somewhere deep in her lungs before it poured out, and she raised her hand and brought it down on the charm.

It cracked, and Marco was in motion again. He must have seen Ty because he became startled and tumbled backwards, said something like, "Where'd you come from?", before Ty leapt towards him and threw him through the motel wall and into the room next to theirs.

Diamond was already on Ty. She had him by the shirt, pushed off into the air, and slammed into the parking lot, cracking the ground but only making him laugh as he coughed his breath back.

"*Don't*," she hissed softly. "I understand what it's like to not have your father's approval—"

"Oh, shut up!" he snapped and forced her off of him with his knees, where she landed on her back as her dad came flying out of the motel and landed a punch in Ty's jaw that sent him back a couple steps.

All around them, people were coming out of their rooms. There was quite the commotion; a lot of lights turning on, people asking questions, and someone said, "What the hell's going on here?". Diamond yelled for everyone to get back inside while Ty landed two good punches in Barry's stomach before he spun around, grabbed him by the back of the neck, and dropped down into a sitting position so that Barry's chin bounced off Ty's shoulder.

Barry should have been stronger. He should have been able to take Ty all by himself, but since he lost hope...Was that it? Was he so hopeless that he had no place from which to draw strength?

It was right then that Marco flew out of the room in which he'd been thrown. His wings came out and flapped in circles, creating a gasp that spread amongst the onlookers and a whirlwind that picked Ty up long enough for Diamond to tackle him, land two punches in his cheek before Ty somersaulted, grabbed hold of her, and threw her into the ground.

"Do none of you know who my father is?" Ty asked. "You think you can take me?"

"Oh, screw your father!" Diamond snarled, grunting as she got up. "I've hung around enough rejects and barflies to know a narcissistic sadist when I see one, and he's playing you like, you know—a fiddle."

"A moral crusader, too," Ty replied mockingly. "How attractive. Hopefully your new boyfriend likes it."

Marco went to say something, but Ty moved so fast he was nothing more than a blur before his fist collided with Marco's face and knocked him out completely. Diamond rushed towards him before he smashed the back of his head off the ground, then eased him into a supine position while Ty laughed somewhere behind her.

"Cute," he said. Then, to Barry, who was just getting up, "You gonna come with me or what?"

"Not on your life," Barry hissed, shaking off the last remnants of the move Ty'd used on him earlier. "It's gonna take more than that to put me down—"

Ty was much stronger and faster than she ever thought he'd be. And whatever demonic part of him was in there, the part that overwhelmed the human part, the human part that was now not only abused by his own father but heartbroken and betrayed by a woman she was sure he was coming to love—that demonic part of him laughed as he put Barry down one last time.

There was nothing Diamond could do to help. She didn't even have a chance to make a move before something like a portal opened up behind Ty, who dragged her father inside and disappeared. All she could do now was scream and pound her fists into the pavement, even as all around her cell phone pictures were being taken and now, for sure, people knew that there were things out there that they'd only dreamed of, and this was gonna get out to the rest of the world—but even *that* she couldn't think of, nor could she think of Marco who was getting to his feet and clutching the back of his head, which bled onto his fingertips.

What was she gonna do now? A car pulled up into the parking lot and shone its headlights on her. She held her hand up to shield her eyes as the doors opened and closed, and two silhouetted figures approached from either side of the car.

She shook her head. "You're too late. They already got him."

Mrs. Delphine placed a hand on her shoulder. Lucas, meanwhile, helped Marco to his feet, threw his friend's arm over his shoulder, and carried him to the backseat where he laid him down gently.

"Get in," Mrs. Delphine said. "We've got someplace we need to be."

Chapter 14

The stars rushed past her. She was leaning with her head out the window, unable to close her eyes, but instead staring up at the light-speckled sky. There were voices in the car, urgent ones that spoke in fast clips, argued and reargued, but about what she had no idea because Ty's face was sucked into her brain like a parasite that played in short clips again and again—how did he feel in that moment? How far along was he in sacrificing Barry—her dad—to start the end of the world?

Mrs. Delphine's plan better work. It was just that there was this terrible oppressive feeling, this sense that every last option was running out; that she'd blown her cover; that the Angel Of Death couldn't be an option; and that she'd only had her dad back for a short amount of time—could she really get out of this one? What if this new plan didn't work out either?

But of course it'd work out. Abaddon had to have a weakness. And if anyone could find it, Diamond was the go-to girl.

"Everything's gonna be fine," Mrs. Delphine said. "Just keep breathing. We're gonna be there soon."

She must have meant the mansion—they were coming up to the turn. Diamond remembered this. There was a big tree coming up, kind of a lonely tree at the intersection. She'd just have to muster up the energy somehow, find some way to regain positivity, to—

They blew past the intersection. At first she figured, well, maybe she was mistaken, but there was that tree, the big oak tree that was on her left and now behind them. She took a second, her mind raced around trying to figure out what had just happened, and she said, "You missed it."

"Missed what?" Delphine asked.

"The turn. It was back there."

"We're not—the turn to where?"

"To the mansion. Right? We're gonna get my dad back; stop the end of the world."

The silence that followed was thick enough that someone could swim in it. Lucas and Delphine gave each other a look like something had gone terribly awry, and even Marco, recovering, sat up as if flushed with a sudden rush of adrenaline.

"What's going on?" Diamond asked. "Stop the car. Turn around."

"I'm trying to keep us alive," Delphine insisted.

"Okay, so you have another plan to stop Abe from opening the portal. Right?"

"Nothing can stop him. Not you, not me—"

"Then we use the Angel of Death. It's the only option."

"We went through this," Marco said, exasperation rising in his voice. "There's no way of using him without getting you killed."

"Then what the hell are we doing? Where are we going? For the love of God, will somebody just tell me *something*?!"

Mrs. Delphine paused for a moment. She wet her lips, peered up into the rearview, and said, "There's a shelter. It's about an hour away. We're gonna hole up there and regroup."

"You're kidding me."

"In sports terms," Lucas said, "we're 'punting.'"

"Yeah, well I never liked sports. Stop the car, I'm getting out."

"I don't think you understand," Delphine said. "If we go to that mansion, we're gonna die. If we wanna live and give our side a fighting chance, we're gonna have to wait out the invasion, find Little Johnnie, and get the process started to ending this as quickly as possible."

Diamond groaned. "We can end it *now*; we just have to go to that mansion and stop Abaddon ourselves."

"You know," Lucas said, "ever since the whole 'Night Adder fiasco', you've had this chip on your shoulder—"

"Shut up," Diamond spat. "I'm not in the mood. Let me out, or I'm gonna rip the door off."

Lucas opened his mouth to come back with something else, and her patience drained completely. She flung her wings out and blasted the door open, rolled out, and let her wings catch her before she scraped her face along the pavement. By the time she landed on her feet, the car squealed to a halt behind her, followed by a din of voices.

Come on, she wasn't listening anymore. The only thing she wished was that she'd brought a jacket, because it was gonna be a cold little flight all the way to the mansion.

Although, she had to admit—and for a city girl, this was no small thing—the countryside *did* look stunning at night. Maybe it was the flatness of it, how open everything looked; the creepy little barns in the distance...It was just death-like and eerie enough that the goth in her relaxed, felt itself drawn and intrigued.

Oh well. At least she'd have all that before she went back into that godforsaken mansion to save the world again.

She planted her feet, squatted down a ways, and pulled her wings back when Marco said, "Wait. Just a second, please."

She rolled her eyes. It was a juvenile response, but it came naturally, and she faced him and held out her arms. "What?"

"You can't use the Angel of Death," he said. "*Please*."

"First off, you're wasting my time. Second, I always find a way out of these things, so you're being ridiculous."

"One time. *One time* you found a way to beat the bad guy, and now you act like this whole thing's second nature."

"*Everyone* has a weakness. If I can find Abaddon's, I'll use it against him. If he doesn't, I'll get Azrael, and I'll find some way through to convincing him not to take me. There, you happy?"

"No." Marco stepped forward and held his hand out. "We're going to this shelter no matter what. Do you know what that means?"

Her mouth went dry. She tried to swallow, but there was nothing there.

"It means we're not gonna help you get yourself killed. It means, by the way, that we plan on living and continuing the fight once it's safe to do so. But all this sounds to you like we're abandoning you, doesn't it? Because you're so sure you can pull this off when, by the way, you can't—"

"*Yes*...I *can*."

"Or you're so blinded by the fact that that's your father out there that you're willing to let everyone else down to get him back. To put yourself at risk—hell, to put the *world* at risk."

"Are you *done*?"

"No," Marco said. By now, he was only a few feet away from her and reaching for her hand. "I don't want you to go because I don't wanna watch you die. Because I'm in love with you."

She'd never known what it was like to have her breath taken away, but that was what happened to her. Sure, she'd known that he felt that way about her—she even felt that way about him, she was sure—but hearing the words spoken was like being hit with something really, *really* heavy.

It confirmed everything she'd suspected about him. And in that moment, a vision flashed, of her getting back into the car, of holing up with the three of them, of being close to Marco. Of them staying alive and returning to fix what had gone wrong in the meantime, and everything turning out happy in the end.

But that was her father out there. And he didn't have to die because she could save him. Especially not at the hands of another man she loved, one she'd betrayed but, you know, even that—that could be fixed too, couldn't it? If she left with Marco, the amount of wreckage she would have left behind—not just what had happened with Ty, and not just the life of a dad she never knew, but the whole world would become one giant ash-heap.

She grabbed hold of Marco's hand by the fingers and squeezed. He squeezed back in a way that suggested he thought he'd convinced her, and for the first time since she could remember, her eyes grew wet. It was right as she pulled away from him, and he gasped, saying something like, "Don't," but she was already up in the clouds.

She'd show them. She'd show them all. In a few hours, she'd have this whole mess cleaned up, and they'd be telling her they'd been wrong, that they wished they would have come with her. They'd see.

She'd show them.

***

Not again. Not again, for the love of God why did he have to be here *again*...His skin crawled. He—did he scream? There were chants all around him, a symphony of deep voices that chilled his heart. He must have screamed. He *must* have. Why else did his voice hurt? What else could he have done while he was thrashing around, bruising his ankles and wrists against the restraints that kept him down on this cold, steel table, while faces stared at him without a care in the world, darkened by the hoods that covered them...the purple hoods with the gold trim. Was it a vision? Was it real?

He pulled as hard as he could on the restraints, and they clanked and rattled against themselves but that was all; they wouldn't move they—they wouldn't budge, nor break, nor...

"Let me out of here!" Barry screamed. "Somebody help me!"

An angel crying—was he the first? His mind was snapping, the darkness massaged it into a goopy mess. The tall, black figure that stood before him; he was the one responsible, he was the one who'd gone into his brain and mashed it into a pulp. Barry screamed again and pulled on the chains, trying to grab hold of Abaddon before anything worse than this happened, but Abaddon was unfazed. He didn't care. And why should he? He was the one with the giant blade, the one that would open Barry up in front of the ring behind him. The one that would finish the ritual and let the evil out into the world, the evil that would consume everything; that would bring goodness down to its knees.

It couldn't get any worse than this. It couldn't. Abe approached him from the side and placed a hand on the back of Barry's head. The droning chants continued, maybe getting louder, it was so hard to tell, and Barry shook and tried to get Abaddon's hand away from him, but it was no use. Abe held on tight, grabbing the hair on the back of his head and lifting the glinting blade into the air.

"Bringer of darkness," Abaddon said, "we wrest from this being his life to give unto thee, O Dark One, behind whom trails the Plagues that will crush humanity—"

"Let me go," Barry pleaded. His voice was small now, weak. "What do you want me to do? You want me to find you another angel, huh? I'll do it. I don't care anymore, I just can't take the darkness, it's clinging to my insides..."

It really was. It was like oil, filling up inside of him until it wrapped its claws around his heart and squeezed. It had been years of this. Years of this presence, crushing him, berating him, rendering him a shadow, a skeleton, a nothing...a nobody. And now it was back. Hollowness. Uselessness. Pointlessness. Like someone shoveling dirt all over you, the cold, the graininess.

His tears wouldn't move anyone in this room. There was no amount of begging or pleading or change of plans that could convince any of these *things* of anything. He only closed his eyes as the blade was drawn up into the air, as the chanting definitely got louder this time, and a wail came out of his mouth, a wordless cry that was sent out into the empty aether to a crowd that didn't care and never would.

This was it. The pain that was coming. It signaled not just the end of his life—it signaled the end of *everything*. All it would take was one drop of blood on the altar. But Abaddon wouldn't stop at one drop, would he?

Then, without warning, came a sound, a *thud*...

And the ground shook.

Chapter 15

Diamond landed in front of the mansion with a 'thud' loud enough that it should let everyone know she was here—which was kind of the plan. She'd already wasted enough time arguing with the others, so she had no idea how far along they were in there, and she hoped this would put enough of a panic in them that they'd at least have to change their timeline.

Which was doubly good, because there was something in her that wanted her paralyzed. Maybe it was fear—her heart was pumping awfully fast, and she was sure there was sweat on her palms. Or maybe it was something else, some other part of her; the part that replayed the conversation with Marco about not wanting to watch her die.

She had no time for this. She breathed deep and pushed herself towards the door, at which point she pulled her leg up and her hip back and kicked right at the center of the door, throwing it open and into the anteroom.

There was no one here. They must have been in the basement. She still remembered where that was, so she ran, putting everything she could into running towards the dining room, where she'd find the door to the basement on the other side, when a shape appeared in the doorway in front of her.

There wasn't enough light to see who it was, but the sense of a brick wall landing in front of her was all she needed to know, and she collided with this object and was sent backwards, toppling over herself until she skidded across the floor. She shook her head to get the cobwebs loose.

Of course, she already knew who it was. Ty stood over top of her, his face in a scowl. He cracked his knuckles and rotated his shoulders, taking a step towards her, but slowly, carefully.

"Who is he?" Ty growled. "The other boyfriend?"

"Jealousy's a gross emotion, by the way."

"You don't think I feel gross? I opened up to you, and that's not easy for me. And you—didn't you feel something?"

"There's a shelter," Diamond said. "I can take you there."

"Changing the subject—"

"No, I'm answering you. I know this demon part of you is mad—don't laugh. I've got demons in my own way, and I know what it's like to lose control. How good it feels. How much you wanna take that out on everyone else."

"That's not the same."

"Isn't it?" Diamond tried to get up, but he made a move like that wasn't a good idea, and she remained still. "I'm saying you don't have to be like this. I've seen the goodness in you."

"Are you gonna leave your boyfriend, then? Is that the plan; that you and I come to this shelter, and I fight for the good guys and we fall in love?"

"It could be."

"That's not good enough." He bent down in front of her so that his body took up the entirety of her vision. "I want your word that you're not gonna be with him. Because *why*? Because what do you think I'm gonna do if I'm stuck in some bomb shelter with the woman I love—and she's with another man?"

"That's the demon talking again," she said. "It's not you."

"I don't think you understand. My mother wasn't just someone whom my dad took advantage of—she was a half-blood, just like you. There's a quarter angel in me. And I've been fighting my entire life to get that side of me to shut up."

She rested her forehead on the ground. Had she misread him the entire time? Was his conflict really against the goodness in him? Or was this just him caving into the darkness?

"And now that I know there's a shelter around here somewhere," he said, "once I'm done with you, I'm gonna scour every square inch of this terrain until I find your friends, and I'm gonna kill all of them. And if your boyfriend's there, he's gonna wish he'd never fallen in love with the same girl as me."

"You think I made a mistake?"

"I *know* you did."

"Well," she said, "I guess we should find out."

She pushed herself up and spun as quickly as she could, sending Ty skidding back on his heels until she dropped into a standing position, her fists in front of her, at the ready. His face was—well, interesting in that moment; something like cockiness rested there but something else as well, like pain and fear; maybe *regret*. He cracked his neck and balled his own hands into fists, but the quivering in his lip told her everything she needed to know; that he didn't wanna do this any more than she did.

There was a chance for him yet. She planted her feet firmly and squared her jaw. "Last chance. All you have to do is get out of my way."

"You'll have to kill me."

Fine. With a yell, she leapt into the air, grabbed hold of the overhang above the doorway, and flung her feet outwards to meet him in the chest. He grabbed hold of her ankles and threw her into the dining room, where she landed on the table, sending a couple plates crashing over the edge.

That was a pretty good move. But now he was coming towards her, so she kicked herself off the table and onto her feet just in time to sidestep him, wrap herself around his leg, get behind him, and bounce his head off the table. It left a good-sized crack that stunned him long enough she could kick the back of his knees, buckle his leg, and land a punch to the back of his head.

"Dammit," he snarled. "Where'd you learn that?"

"None of your—"

But that was just a distraction...and it worked. A split second later, he spun around with a roundhouse that landed in her stomach and finished with an elbow to the back of her neck that she was sure was gonna knock her head clean off. All of this put her in a good position to grab him by the waist, lift him up, and smash his back down onto the table; lift him up again and smash him one more time, this time right through the table.

Before he could get up, she grabbed one of the wooden chairs, flipped it like a home run hitter with a bat, grabbed it with both hands, and smashed it down on him just as he put both his arms up to block it.

Which was when all hell broke loose. She grabbed him by the ankle now and dragged him out of the wreckage, but he screamed and shot up into the air, a guttural roar poured out of his lungs, and before she knew what hit her, she was on the ground getting pummeled, the bottoms of his fists landed again and again, too fast for her to get her arms up to block.

It was he who stopped himself. Her vision was failing, the gold-speckled ceiling swirled and churned, spit dangled out of her mouth, and Ty paced around cursing, saying, "Why did you make me do this? Huh? *Why*!?"

"I didn't..."

She spat blood. This was getting bad. She was shaking, wobbling as she got herself to her feet, then stumbled backwards. She wasn't in fighting condition; whatever he'd done to her had nearly put her out, nearly *killed* her.

And he didn't have a scratch on him.

How was she gonna beat him? She closed her eyes and breathed a moment, feeling her wings flutter against her back. This was her only chance, as far as she could tell—she'd have to unload hell on him.

Maybe he was gonna say something then. It certainly looked like it, but she didn't give him a chance. With a yell as loud as any she could muster, she flew towards him, sending out her wings in a flurry that grabbed hold of his skin, cut, yanked, and pushed; she didn't let him fall down, but in a blurry fashion, battered and slashed at him until he fell to his knees, his face bleeding and his chest, arms, and everything else bleeding as well.

He held up his hand for her to stop, but she'd come too far now. She kicked him in the face like she was kicking a football, caught him as he shot up into the air from the force of the hit, and rushed towards the far wall, over by where the door to the basement was where she unloaded on him again, using her elbows and knees this time, aware suddenly that tears formed in her eyes; that she wasn't just screaming in violence but in terror, that she was *killing* him, and she didn't want to at all. She wanted to stop; she wanted to be somewhere else, *anywhere* else...

Finally, he yelled, "Stop!", and she did.

He used the wall to prop himself up. She stepped back, sobbing, wanting to take everything back but not knowing how. He was catching his breath—heaving with each new inhale, his lungs rattling, no doubt from inhaling blood.

"Are you through?" she asked, choking through a sob.

"No." He shook his head. "I'm not. You?"

"No." Which was a lie. But she was sure it was coming from him, too, because he buckled and had a hell of a time standing straight.

"You should have stayed with me," he said. "We would have never had to do this, you know. And once the next world comes—"

"Why are you still pretending?!" Her voice came out almost in a scream. "Who's this for, huh? Nobody's watching but me."

"You're wrong. I'm not good. You've seen where I come from—"

"You tried to save my dad. What do you call *that*?"

"Weakness."

His shoulders tensed. Now she cursed this time, knowing what was coming, and planted her feet just as she did before; made fists just as she did before, holding them out in front of her. Only this time, her wings came out of her back and flexed in front of him, as though even they hoped that a display of strength would be enough, that she wouldn't have to do the real thing.

She was wrong—the wings were wrong. Ty pushed himself off from the wall and threw a punch at her that missed horribly. She grabbed him from under his arm and pressed upwards with one hand and down with the other, dislocating his shoulder. He yelped and threw the other hand at her, which she grabbed by the wrist and threw him over her own shoulder in a Judo move that had him lying on the ground.

He tried to roll over, to get himself up, but she kicked him in the lower back. His body recoiled. He grabbed at where she'd hit him, and she knew that was a weak spot, so she wound up and hit him again, her face dry from tears now, as though there were no more she could spare.

Finally, he lay still. His breathing was labored. The pain must have been *excruciating*.

She couldn't help herself. She fell down at his side and placed a hand on either side of his bloodied head and found what was left of her tears when she said, "I'm sorry," and kissed him, his blood wetting her lips.

He tried to speak. She drew nearer, pressing her ear against his shivering lips as close as she could without suffocating him until finally the words came:

"No, you're not," he said. "Not yet."

Even he didn't believe in her. Which didn't matter at this point. The rage that boiled up in her was almost too much for her to handle. She wiped the tears from her eyes, the snot from her nose, and got up, walking towards the basement door.

The chanting came through the door from up the stairs. She was almost there. Only one more step, and she was gonna save the world.

Chapter 16

The chanting grew louder. Was that what made her shiver on the way down? Already she was growing exhausted. Her limbs hurt from fighting Ty, and yes, she was shivering, but it wasn't cold; it was warm.

She recited, mentally, the prayer Barry had taught her: "O come Angel of Death, that ye may tip the scales to good and take this soul to the world after." Was she gonna need it? No, she wouldn't need it. She could find Abe's weakness, whatever it was—some allergy to something, a physical weak spot, a mental blind spot, *anything*. He had to have one. He *had* to.

She reached the bottom of the stairs. The portal was just where it had been last time: to the right of the desk with all the monitors hooked up to surveillance cameras, with souvenirs taken from Abe's exploits throughout history scattered about the whole place. The difference was that now, around the portal, was a troupe of hooded figures, no doubt his servants—no doubt Roy—and they were standing over a metal slab which was obscured from her view by their bodies.

One thing stood out, however: it was Abe, taller than the rest, wearing a robe as well but holding a knife in the air, ready to bring it down.

She was almost too late. Two more seconds and Abe would have—but she couldn't think about that. There was a glass case with weapons next to her, old Medieval ones like a morning star, which was a kind of staff with a spiked ball fixed to the end of it. It was just what she needed. She smashed the glass case with her elbow, pulled the morning star out, extended her wings, and pushed off from the ground, flying towards Abe with both hands wrapped around the mace and yelling as loud as she could.

He didn't see her coming. She brought the spiked end of the morning star into the side of his head and made him lose his balance.

The sacrificial dagger flew out of his hand and clanked on the ground while she caught her footing and he checked his face for blood.

He found none.

"Your timing's impeccable," he said, his mouth not moving. "You only had another second."

"I've always been punctual." She gripped the morning star tighter as the hooded figures stopped chanting and turned towards her. She took a step back, and her heel touched the back wall—she had nowhere to go but *through* them. Abaddon was on the other side, confident, smiling at her.

And where was her dad? On the other side of this wall of bodies, likely the source of the clanking-of-chains sound she could hear over the rustling of cloth as the robed men drew nearer.

"We don't have to do it like this," she said. "It's up to you if you wanna live—or not."

"You're relying on hubris? Where are your friends, I wonder? Why have you come alone? Is it because they've abandoned you?"

"No offense to them, but I like my chances. Are we doing this or not?"

He didn't have to make a move one way or another. The crowd of hooded servants plunged towards her like a horde of zombies, and without thinking, she extended her wings, held the morning star out from herself, and spun around as quickly as she could. The morning star caught the crowd and dragged through them, tossing them out of her way while others grabbed hold of her, trying to slow her down.

Their plan worked, but only for the moment. The weight of the horde on her shoulders, as they piled on top of her, made one of her knees buckle until her wings lashed out, taking out one after the other while she growled and forced them off of her, swinging the morning star again and again, colliding with bodies and faces, building onto the pile that accumulated in front of her.

She threw one more off of her and into the wall behind. There were a few more left, including Roy, and they were coming for her, but there was a space opened up for her now. Abaddon was right there, and she pushed herself off the ground and swung the morning star, aiming right underneath his chin—but he caught her by the wrist and held her in front of him, with her feet dangling off the ground while the morning star fell from her grip and landed with a 'thud'.

Panic—that was what she felt. She wriggled and writhed, tried to get out from his grasp, but he only laughed at her. He lifted her up until their eyes met, and his voice came into her mind, saying, "You're better than I thought you'd be," before hurling her into the ground.

Two of the hooded figures grabbed her from underneath her arms and held her in place. Roy did the same, pressed down onto her shoulders while Abaddon grabbed hold of the knife, and for the first time, she saw her dad, the insanity in his eyes and the screaming that was taking all of his energy.

Her wings shot out and killed the two men on both sides of her. It scared Roy off so that he let go and backed up, which let Diamond spin around and send a kick right into the side of his head that knocked him unconscious, sprawled him out—or so it looked like. She didn't give herself even a second to make sure as she leapt onto Abe's back and wrapped her arms around his neck, desperately squeezing, hoping that she could cut his air off but finding his throat as stiff as an oak tree.

"Are you trying to choke me?" he laughed and pushed himself backwards to crush her against the concrete wall behind them. Her body cracked the material and something, oh God, *something* was wrong with her back if he hit her like that again—

She let go before he crushed her completely. Her left leg—she couldn't quite move it; it limped, it was like the blood had been cut off. And he thought this was funny, the bastard. He wound up and brought his fist down like an avalanche into the side of her head, so everything went black for a moment.

God, there was nothing like getting hit by this man. Another punch came, and she went down to her knees just before he landed a kick in her chest that crippled her, sucking the breath out of her lungs.

She wheezed, heaving violently. Every bone, every muscle in her body hurt. She couldn't beat him. He had no weakness. And now he was laughing maniacally to himself, chanting, bringing the dagger up while Barry's eyes went wild, and he screamed like his brain was ready to snap completely.

What else could she do? Some of that confidence came back. She breathed. The prayer—it was the only thing left. And she was sure—Azrael would see reason, wouldn't he?

She clutched her hands into fists. Abaddon's back was facing her; he held the dagger up above his head. If she was gonna make a move, she was gonna do it *now*. She'd have to. With a yell, she made one last leap onto Abaddon's back, grabbed hold of his neck again, ignoring how funny he thought this whole arrangement was, and said into his ear so he could hear her, "O come Angel of Death, that ye may tip the scales to good and take this soul to the world after," just as he brought the knife down—

But he stopped himself and threw her off him, turning around to face her. For the first time, his eyes showed fear. It was her turn to laugh.

"What'd you do?" he asked, sheer terror in his voice.

"Didn't you hear me?" She smiled through her bloodied teeth.

"But—that means..."

Her breath turned to condensation. The shivering grew worse. From where was this coming? Had the entire world changed in that one second, had everything become so—what? *Nothing*?

She backed up until she was against the wall. Abaddon must have seen it, too. His eyes glanced around at the cellar, and he repeated the word "No", like he was doing so unconsciously. She couldn't help herself. She crouched down and wrapped her arms around her knees, and for a second, she was gonna cry, but the sadness was replaced by something much, much *worse.*

Was this always the way things were? Was everything just one big nothing? Were her hands just flesh and bone, ligaments pulled like puppet strings by neurons that fired without her control? But even that sensation gave way to something else, something deeper; something that grew increasingly beyond her ability to describe it.

Eventually, there were no words. Nothing she could say or think that measured up to the blackness, the nothingness that came over her. Everything seemed frozen, covered in dirt and endlessly cold. If she found herself lying with her cheek against a dry skull, she wouldn't have been surprised—but here there was no such thing as 'surprise'. There was no emotion to accompany any of it.

It was death.

A rasping breath echoed throughout the cellar. At the far end, in the shadows, a shape stirred. Each movement was like bones being dropped onto the floor, every breath like that of a cancer patient. It moved towards them, but how it moved was difficult to tell, and that it moved *so* slowly...

Should she run? Why was her jaw hanging open like this? Abaddon dropped his knife and held his hands up as the shade came upon him; a black, wispy thing that crawled out of the darkness and reached for him, leaving a trail of ice and dust in its wake.

"I don't wanna go," Abaddon said. "Please, I need more time..."

The shade touched his head—with *what* she couldn't say, but it touched him, and all at once, Abaddon coughed and grew weak, while black tendrils wrapped around him like chains. He screamed and tried to pry himself loose, but he couldn't; there was no getting away from whatever this thing was—this dark, inevitable thing.

Why didn't the cold make her shiver anymore? She'd lost all hope now of reasoning with this thing, because whatever it was, it was beyond reason; beyond *understanding*, even. It was a thing without concern that rose from its grave-like abode and senselessly brought all movement, all hope, everything down to the level of nothingness.

It was because of this that when its tendrils wrapped around her, she didn't speak. She pulled against it, but more out of instinct than out of any conscious effort to resist. Her will was broken down. She couldn't even force herself to move a muscle, but her mouth formed words beyond her control:

"Wait," she said, echoing Abaddon's words, "I need more time..."

The Angel of Death pulled her towards the shadows it came here from. In front of her, Abaddon became a slow-moving, molasses person, eventually succumbing to the entropy that was all around them. Azrael, meanwhile, the wispy shade of death, pulled him towards and into the darkness, and he disappeared one step at a time, without putting up anything like a fight.

This would happen to her, too. She had nothing left, no energy. She could *barely* walk. And something about the entrance into the next world seemed so comforting—

But before she could leave this world behind, something stopped her. It wasn't her; she hadn't regained her willpower or anything like that. It was something outside of her, something holding on. But what—

It was a hand, one on both shoulders. And whoever's hands they were, they were pulling her away from the dark.

"Let go of her!" the voice shouted. "She's not going with you!"

Who was it? She recognized the face, even though it was bloody, swollen, and bruised. It was—good God, it was Ty! He was digging his heels into the ground; they were literally *digging* into the ground, and the wispy shape changed into something approximating anger and hissed at him.

"She's coming with me," the whispering voice said. "That's the trade..."

"That's not a fair trade," Ty responded. "She did nothing—me, I'm the one who screwed up. Take me."

The wispy tendrils let go of Diamond, and she fell onto her hands and knees. It was like she breathed for the first time in years, but the dustiness of the Angel of Death still filled her lungs, and she coughed, wiping the wetness out of her eyes.

This couldn't be happening. Azrael wrapped itself around Ty, and he took on that now-familiar expression of a being without will. His face went even paler, and his eyes glazed over as he marched zombie-like towards the blackness.

This wasn't how it was supposed to go. She screamed and grabbed hold of him, but Azrael's shadow-body swatted her away and pulled him into the dark.

"Hold on," she begged. "Please, I can explain. Getting rid of Abaddon was a good idea, but you don't have to take someone else—"

"You're not the first person to try and reason with death," Azrael said. "Guess how many have been successful? This man is a suitable sacrifice to take the life of Abaddon—something you can't live without, child."

Ty's body was disappearing into the shadows. She screamed and thrust her wings out into Azrael's oily body but only hit air, like he was made of fog, and even as she tried to grab hold of Ty, he became like air himself and disappeared.

Eventually, in what must have been only seconds, the light came back into the dark room. Diamond didn't notice it at first; she was consumed by suffering of her own kind, beating her fist against the ground. Why couldn't she save him?! Wasn't the plan to stop the invasion and save Ty from his father? Why did she fail?!

But she hadn't failed completely. She got herself up to standing and faced her father, who was breathing heavily on his steel slab, looking weak and unstable. He was still gritting his teeth, even, so she approached him and placed a hand on his head. "It's alright, it's over."

Using her wings, she broke him free of the chains before helping him to his feet. His shaking was terrible. She put herself under his shoulder to help carry him, thinking past her own limp, her own injuries, but still sliding along the ground while she tried to get her bad leg working.

This was gonna take a while. And for whatever reason, Barry kept trying to say something, but it wouldn't come out...?

"You can tell me later," she whispered. "We have to get a move on."

"You don't understand." It took everything he had to get himself to speak. "We have to leave here *now*."

What did he—but why? Sweat poured down his face. His skin trembled and shook, his shoulder—well, his shoulder seemed to be...Bleeding...

That was the moment she was sure her heart stopped beating. The steel slab he'd been laying on had just the slightest hint of blood on it, but it was there, and right up above it a swirling collection of light and dark swam together in one whole, filling the portal and creating the gateway.

Sparks flew out of it. Lightning crashed somewhere. And a skeletal hand reached through the swirl of light, coming from some other world.

She and her father ran as fast as they could. Within minutes, the portal had grown to an unfathomable size, and an army of darkness had walked through to bring literal Hell on Earth.

Chapter 17

Only a couple hours after the portal opened, Diamond sat hiding in an abandoned barn while all around her chaos erupted. She could feel every death, every wound, every loss. It was as though someone were stabbing her again and again, relentlessly, without hesitation or concern.

Barry peered out through one of the barn windows. What did he see out there? She couldn't make out his expression past the tears in her eyes, but he wasn't moving, wasn't recoiling in shock or anything of the sort.

How could he be so unfazed? Had they really busted him up *that* bad?

"What are you gonna do?" Barry asked.

Diamond wiped snot away with the back of her hand and caught her breath. "I don't know. Find my friends, I guess. Hope that I haven't screwed up so bad that they don't wanna talk to me anymore. And as long as there's two of us—"

"There won't be. I'm not coming with you."

She shook her head in disbelief, pressed her hand into the hay behind her, and stood up. Now that the tears were dry, she could see the coldness of his expression, the stony selfishness he wore.

"You can't convince me," he said. "We can't win. You haven't looked outside yet, to see what they're doing. It's coming our way, too, so we'll wanna get a move on from here."

"What are you gonna do, then? Hide?"

"Survive."

"What a buncha crap. What a bunch of—I know a Medicine Man; we can get through this."

"Still haven't learned your lesson, huh? This attitude of yours is what got you into this mess. If you'd just let me die—"

"I thought I could beat him."

"Exactly. You 'thought'. And look what happened."

She didn't have to think hard to know that he was right. Losing Ty was her fault. But keeping Ty would have meant losing her dad, whom she'd just gotten to know after years of thinking they'd never meet.

The unfairness—that was the killer here, wasn't it? She was suffering because of her hubris, just like Abaddon had told her. And she'd almost gotten herself killed in the process, which hadn't been lost on her. The only reason she was alive was because of luck.

But she couldn't let her dad abandon her like this, not when she needed him the most.

"I know that look," he said. "And listen, I get it. I've seen your people start off young and stupid, and most of them, frankly, *stay* stupid. But you don't have to, you know. You can make the smart move. You can recognize that there are no guarantees in this world; that you might not come out on top this time, and that means abandoning whatever 'Save The World' project you wanna embark on and making sure you stay alive."

"With you? Are you asking me to go *with you*?"

"No. I'm going it alone. But if you're smart, so will you."

She didn't have the energy to convince him otherwise. She couldn't even look at him as he walked past her, through the barn doors, and out into the world. It was minutes, maybe longer before she looked out through the fields, to the fire that was consuming the little town on the horizon, the screaming from the people there growing louder.

Was he wrong? What were the odds of being successful when the adversary was this powerful? And that she hadn't even encountered the most powerful enemies yet, the Dark Ones—what would she be willing to give up for that, when she'd given *everything* this time?

Maybe the only thing left really *was* survival.

***

What happened over the months after the portal opened is almost beyond description. The armies of the world amassed as quickly as they could, but they were just as quickly put down. Many of the leaders of these armies were made examples of in the most sadistic, evil ways imaginable. Once these punishments were made public, there was a rash of resignations, of military and political leaders pledging allegiance to the new masters of the world.

Resistance movements were quashed. Anyone who spoke out in public was found and destroyed. The world over became nothing but suffering. People were torn from their homes. And try as anyone could to find a reason for all this, a goal that these creatures had in mind, the suffering seemed to be its own reward. They were *truly* beyond persuasion. And as Diamond saw the infinite parade of horrors that traveled across the world—and the ease with which resistance was crushed—it dawned upon her more and more that maybe Barry was right. The only thing she could do in a world like this was try to live, even as it became increasingly likely that that wouldn't be for much longer. Nobody lived forever in a world like this. Nobody.

Not that far away, Marco stood at the edge of the ladder that led down into the shelter, while above him enormous objects stamped across the entrance that was hidden and thick enough to withstand the kind of beating that came from the end of the world.

But for how much longer?

"They'll find us eventually," Marco said.

"We're fine," Lucas reassured him, coming out of the kitchen with coffees for everyone. There was a little dining room right near the entrance to the shelter, where Mrs. Delphine sat at the small table, shaking her head as if that would make the sound go away. Lucas set the coffees down at the table and took a seat.

"Whose idea was this anyway?" Marco asked. Then to Lucas, "Yours?"

"It'll hold. Come on, what do you take me for? You think I'd put us somewhere that *wasn't* safe?"

"No, I think maybe you'd put us somewhere you *thought* was safe, but it might not be as safe as you think."

Lucas brushed him off. Marco kept focused on the entrance, unsure if it was buckling from pressure, from having all that weight drag across it. It was a whole army of evil, after all; plus any number of vehicles, possibly bombs, by the sounds of it...

"Staring at it isn't gonna make it any better," Lucas said.

Marco almost snapped something back, but Mrs. Delphine said, "Please. We don't know how long we're gonna be here. If you guys can't get along already—"

"I can 'get along,'" Marco said. "I'm just saying, this thing's not gonna last, and we're all gonna get caught."

"Will you tell him?" Lucas asked, and Mrs. Delphine said, "It's my opinion that the shelter can hold."

Now it was Marco who brushed them off, and who ignored Lucas saying, "Thank you. See? We're gonna be fine. Will you sit down, please? Before you make me so nervous I lose my mind?"

Marco sighed and took a seat, but wouldn't make eye contact. There was no way the other two were right, but if they were, he wasn't in any kind of mood to argue. He just picked up his coffee, took a drink, and stared into the wall.

That silence went on for some time. It was Lucas, however, that broke it. "Do we think Diamond made it?"

"I don't wanna talk about it," Marco said. "Can we not talk about it?"

"How are we gonna know? Does she know where to find us?"

"She's a smart girl," Delphine said. "I just suspect—"

She cut herself off. There was a particularly heavy blast that shook the ceiling. Cups rattled in the cupboards. Whatever the rumbling was, it wasn't stopping, either. It just kept going. Even the coffee in Marco's cup made waves that sloshed over the side and onto the ground.

Everyone stood perfectly still. Then it stopped. They all took a breath at the same time.

"See?" Lucas asked. "We're fine."

"What do we think that was?" Marco said back.

"Who cares? Here, I'll get you a napkin—"

The rumbling started again. This time, it was clear that something above them exploded, and it really shook the shelter. Marco even felt it in the soles of his feet.

And judging by the looks everyone wore—

"You guys thinking what I'm thinking?" Marco asked.

Delphine closed her eyes. "Don't say it."

"What about weapons?" Lucas replied. "Where are they?"

"There's a room in the back," Delphine said. "Follow me."

They all stood up, but the second they did, another rumble shook them all to the floor, followed by a terrible explosion as the entrance to the shelter burst downward and smashed into the ground, bounced off and flew towards them in the living room. Marco ducked right at the last second, just before the shelter lid crashed into the wall.

Nobody moved. There were voices coming from somewhere, saying things like, "What's this?"; "Somebody down there?", but maybe if they didn't move, they wouldn't be seen...

"It's a shelter!" a voice said, and that was enough for them. The three of them ran towards the back room as, behind them, the ladder clanked from feet, from people, demons, or something descending.

They went through the living room area to where there was a bookshelf, which Mrs. Delphine fumbled with, pulling books out to find which one would make the secret door open. Marco's pulse was crazy, he could see it in Lucas as well; how Lucas' heart almost pumped out of his neck, and he wanted Delphine to hurry up when—

Four men entered in what looked like SWAT uniforms. Marco and Lucas put their hands up immediately, and Delphine followed only a second later.

"Who are you?" one of the men demanded. "Speak up!"

"We're just people," Marco said. "We thought there was a nuclear war or something so we hid down here."

"Close enough. Any of you angelic?"

Marco swallowed. "No. 'Angelic'?"

"Yeah. Don't screw with me, man. We have ways of telling who might be—Phil, you got that machine?"

One guy to this man's right—Phil—fumbled around for a device he kept on his belt. He was making nervous sounds, like he might have forgotten it.

Was this a 'real' machine? Marco looks to Lucas, who looked to Delphine—what would happen if they found out about Mrs. Delphine? She was *way* too important not to keep alive...

"Alright," Marco said. "Don't worry about the machine. It's me you're looking for, okay?"

"What is he—that's not true," Lucas said. "It's me."

"Well, which one is it?" the man grumbled. "Phil, come on, make with the—"

"It's me," Marco said. "Don't listen to him."

"Alright then," the man said. "You're all coming with us."

"Hold on," Marco said. "But I said—"

"Yeah, yeah, he said-she said, I don't care. We'll take you to someone who'll figure all you guys out. And trust me—you're gonna like him."

Marco's heart sank. He hadn't meant for this to happen. He'd wanted to give the other two a fighting chance. Now all he could do was say "I'm sorry" again and again as they tried to talk him down, to convince him that it was okay. They'd find a way out of this, that Good would prevail...

But it didn't feel like that. It felt like being carried away to death.

Eventually, the ground became like dust. Whoever lived through the initial invasion lived as roving bandits that were eventually caught and destroyed, the survivors thrown into servitude. And somewhere, amongst all of this, Diamond was out there, trying to find hope.

But where?

About the Author

Treena Wynes is a Registered Social Worker with a passion for supporting and unlocking the potential in youth, families and organizations while helping them gain a greater sense of self-awareness. Treena is an international motivational speaker and sees the value in sharing stories as a way to change and save lives. She has won two book awards for her non-fiction book, *Am I The Only One: Struggling Being A Teen.*

Read more at treenawynes.ca.

Milton Keynes UK
Ingram Content Group UK Ltd.
UKHW030822010824
446326UK00001B/49